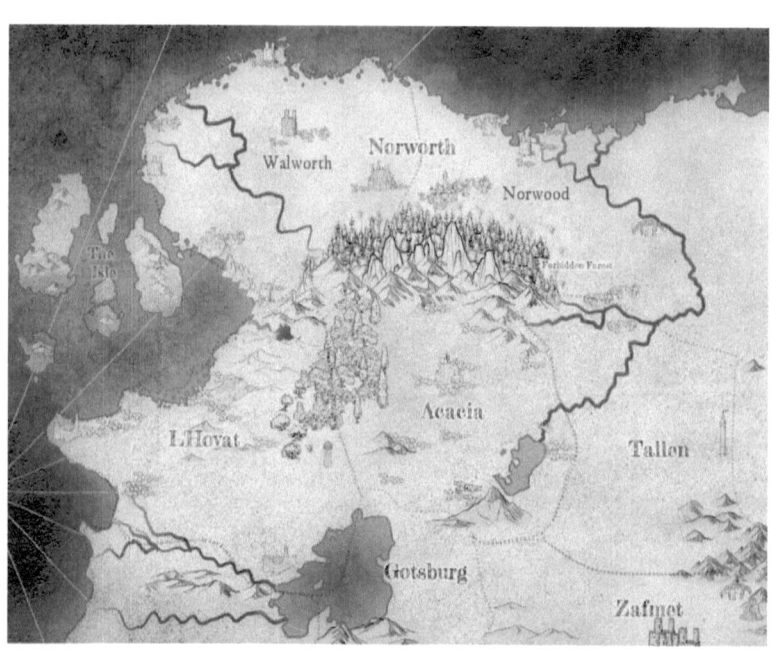

To those who feel like giving up.
Don't.

Tomorrow is coming.

Contents

Trigger Warnings and a Promise from the Author:

While this book is redemptive, Happily Ever After, and contains strong messages of endurance, healing, and hope, there are several potential triggers which I wanted to prepare the reader for. Most are within the Mirror chapters, and so for a light read, one could skip these, trusting they show the root motivations for why the evil queen did such horrible things.

- CHILD ABUSE FROM A PARENT – CHAPTER 2, MIRROR SCENE

- ARRANGED MARRIAGE TO AN ABUSIVE SPOUSE AT 18 – CHAPTER 4, MIRROR SCENE

- NON-CONSENSUAL MARITAL INTIMACY IMPLIED – CHAPTER 4, MIRROR SCENE

- DOMESTIC VIOLENCE – CHAPTER 4 AND CHAPTER 9, MIRROR SCENES

- MENTAL/EMOTIONAL ABUSE SCATTERED THROUGH OTHER MIRROR SCENES.

- BODY OF A MOTHER SHOWN, PREVIOUSLY KILLED BY VIOLENCE (DEATH NOT SHOWN) – CHAPTER 9, MIRROR SCENE

That said, I promise the reader that the horrors are kept as horrors, never glorified, and never rewarded. Justice, forgiveness, and second chances for the victims are provided.

If you are a victim of abuse, please seek counseling and help. You are worthy of protection, love, and safety.

Domestic Violence 24-hour hotline number: 800-799-7233 or, if safe, text: 88788

CHAPTER ONE

The Queen

Present day

Dirty nails and scuffed up knuckles marred her fingers as they held the blood-red apple to her rose-red lips. A puff of flour distorted her porcelain cheek, and I frowned at the filth of the apron covering her ill-fitting frock.

Her treacherous mouth smiled. "It's so beautiful."

Recoiling, I shuffled the fabric back over my basket with my disfigured hand. "Only the fairest apple for the fairest lady."

At the pop from her teeth biting through the skin, my weathered eyes glanced up greedily.

It would all be over soon.

"Why, yes. Oh, thank you!" she twittered. "It's been quite some time since I—" She ahem-ed quietly. "Pardon me. It's been so long since I've had an apple. I had—" She swallowed, her tiny throat bobbing in distress. I restrained a feral grin. Placing a hand to her forehead, she said, "I'm so sorry. I don't feel well."

"Oh, dear me. Have a seat." I pulled a chair over as she shuddered, stepping unsteadily toward it. "Here. For you."

Her eyes glazed over. Her rapid breaths nearly matched mine.

Soon.

"Thank you. I just... Oh my!"

As she collapsed toward the chair, she missed. I could have shifted it to catch her. I could have reached out a hand. But I did not.

She tried to rise and coughed twice. A trickle of blood slipped from her lips, their red hue draining to a bony gray.

Her eyes focused on the round obsidian ring on my left pinky, and her eyes widened in recognition despite my magicked, decrepit appearance. "Mama Kiva?" Her gaze searched my face. "But why?"

Her whole form trembled as I crouched before her. "Why? You were to be a rose, but you are only a thorn, a bramble bush in my beautiful kingdom." She reached for me, and I shuffled back. She fell again; her head hit the floor with a thunk.

I stood slowly, raising my chin as my mother had always taught me. "I am the queen. There can only be one." In the distance, the clop of hooves and creaking wagons approached.

"Mama Kiva," she whispered desperately, fearfully, through those lips that had kissed me, lips that had betrayed me. Her mortal terror threatened my placid composure, but it was too late to stop the poison. This was my curse. My thorn. My salvation.

My freedom lay ahead. I pulled back from her, clenching my fist.

A shuddering gasp. A twitch of her fingers.

Then the princess took her last breath.

I had finally won.

CHAPTER TWO

The Mirror

Twenty-five years earlier

I am the Mirror, and the Mirror is Me.

Objective and cold, I reflect all I see.

No seer nor diviner, though some may still ask.

Only present, never future, though sometimes the past.

I am all mirrors in all places. I see all things. I am the mirror in the bedroom and in the washroom. I am the hand mirrors. I am hung in the royal throne room. I am in the reflections of the poorest hammered metal in the dirt floor huts.

I am the Mirror. But only a few can speak with me.

My columns here in the manor house are shapely and topped with a curl at the center arch. Her four-poster bed is behind her, draped with lace. Her silken sheets are smooth. The room is devoid of toys—nothing to distract from the refined beauty of the furniture. The child, now seven, sits on her velvet stool, brushing her long, curly red hair in my reflection. Fifty-six, fifty-seven, fifty-eight, fifty-nine...

The mother comes to stand behind the girl. Her gown is silk. The magic pearls from her necklace slip through her delicate fingers. Each pearl was once a life, each life taken to extend her own years and to maintain her beauty. Blood magic.

Her brow rises, and she curls her lip. "How many?"

The child flinches.

"How many, Kevali?"

"I-I forgot. F-fifty-one, I think." The child does not ask me, though I know the answer.

The mother strikes the child, and the girl falls forward. She cries out as her forehead hits the corner of the dressing table.

"Start again." The child sits back up, and the mother gathers the girl's hair in her hands. "The hair is the crown for the face. The face is the crown for the body. The woman is the catalyst for the wars that will save our people from this daft king and his fear of magic. I have worked too hard to secure our future. Once Rorin overthrows this sham of a monarchy, and you become his queen, then all magic users will find safety. But you are nothing, without purpose, if you are not beautiful." The mother grabs the child's middle finger and pulls her arm up from her body, dangling it before her. Her lip pinches to the side at the corner, creasing her face. "You are too gangly to be beautiful." She drops the girl's arm.

The child reaches again for the brush. There is water in her eyes and a redness to her cheeks. She begins to brush again. "Yes, Mother."

A thread of blood seeps from the girl's hairline. The mother sucks in a breath and pulls the girl backward by a handful of red hair. "What have you done?" She snatches a handkerchief from the dresser. "Clean it up. Then practice your healing spell to fix your mistake. There can be no scars." The mother throws the fabric at the girl before stalking out of the room in a whirl of silk.

The child's lip trembles as she turns to me, studying herself and watching the water that rises in her eyes, watching the beads of blood from the wound. I am careful to reflect accurately. I take pride in my image, though it is not a beautiful one.

She winds the fabric in her hands. The blood drips onto her cheek now. "Mirror, mirror, on the wall, who is the fairest of them all?"

"Hard and cold as she may be, your mother is the fairest I can see."

The daughter hangs her head. I barely hear her whisper, "Will I ever be enough? Will I ever be loved? When will the fairest be me?"

CHAPTER THREE

The Queen

Present day

My black ring glowed blue at my words, and I watched in glee as the withered, arthritic hands softened back into their long, elegant fingers. In the mirror's reflection, the wrinkly jowls shrunk and tightened. The crows' feet flattened, and the nose shrunk to my usual button tip. The gray eyes bloomed back to their familiar deep blue hue with their almond shape and long lashes. The lips plumped back to rosebuds with an elegant Cupid's bow.

The hair returned last. Wiry white hair exploded into color, bounding over my shoulder into long, curly red lengths. Those locks of hair were what had caught the king's affection, what he held in his hands as he died.

I frowned at the memory before shaking it off.

Today was a day for victory. Today was a day for *me*.

I twisted the ring on my finger, remembering the moment I made it and all it stood for. It was good Snow hadn't noticed it before she accepted the apple. But I had never taken it off. I never would.

Snow.

Snow was dead.

I had lingered, watching, for too long. Waiting for her to suddenly rise again. Waiting for my curse to rebound and for her to undo all I had done. Waiting for the ache in my heart to shift to the joy I had prepared for. Months ago, a soft-hearted huntsman had failed to kill her. This time, I needed to be certain. But the mirror said she breathed no more, and when I held the glass to her mouth, there was no fog. I mirror-portaled to my castle just as the Thwarven men had arrived to the cottage.

Standing, I changed into my blue silk gown; my fingertips followed the wide top, rimmed in emeralds. Pausing before the mirror, I reveled in the beauty of my reflection.

"Mirror, mirror, on the wall, who is the fairest of them all?"

The shadowed form spoke with a thousand voices, as haunting and discordant as ever. "You are," they whispered.

My chest swelled in jubilation, and delicate tears pricked at the corners of my eyes. The emotion flushed my cheeks; the effect was quite lovely.

I had done it.

I was fairest.

I was the queen, and no one could wrest my crown from me.

I struck out down the hall, my head held high and my face serene as I strode between my Black Knights. Their armor glimmered sharply in the torchlight. Yates followed a pace behind me—my butler and constant shadow.

When I was announced to the throne room, the servants and a few nobles bowed low and deep, and I ascended the stairs to the golden seat. When I twisted, Yates adjusted my train before stepping back behind the throne. Ornate large mirrors lined every wall, and small round ones circled every column. I looked regal in their many reflections.

"Snow White is dead." The room, already hushed, fell deathly silent. "She was killed last night. Poisoned." A gasp burst from someone to my left. I glared but was unable to determine the source. The scribes scratched furiously on their parchment. They looked up to me for more words, but I had none.

Sitting down in my chair, I gestured with a wave of my hands. "That is all." The room burst into whispers as people fled—to spread the word, no doubt.

Once it was quiet and only the knights remained, I turned slightly. "Yates."

His old form bustled to my side and dipped to one knee. "Yes, my queen."

"What is the business today?"

Yates pulled at his sleeve, straightening the button. "My queen?"

"I am ready to hold court. Where are the commoners?"

His eyes stayed fixed on his hands. "There are none today."

I turned my shoulders toward him. There had been none last week either. "None?"

He shook his head.

There was a small wave of disappointment before I shut it down. "Must be from my excellent leadership that there are no squabbles or rabble in the masses. Good." Yates blinked, then stepped back into his usual position behind my throne with his head dipped low.

The sun filtered through the brilliant stained-glass windows, highlighting tiny motes of dust. The susurrus of my silk dress rustled too loudly as I tapped the toes of my leather shoes. The silence was deafening.

I was queen. I was beautiful.

I was alone.

Time passed. An uncomfortable itch prickled in my chest.

"Yates?"

Yates bowed. "My queen?"

"Arrange for my carriage. I will ride through Acacia."

"As you wish."

CHAPTER FOUR

The Mirror

Twenty-two years earlier

I am the Mirror, and the visage is true.

What you see in me reflects what I see in you.

Though pretense and wealth are too common a shield.

Her scars mark the weakness she tries to conceal.

I stand behind the fountain, my surface flecked with drops of water from the pool beneath. The wings of the manor house strike out to each side, with a garden in the center. The sky is cloudless. The child, now ten, hides behind a shrub. Her tutor runs by calling for her—calling for Kevali.

The child waits. Then stands. She dances on pointed feet before sitting on the rim of my fountain. Her face turns toward the light of the sun. On the other side, a boy with brown skin, his black curly hair topped with a dark purple velvet hat, walks backward before he turns to run to the flowering bush in the center of the circular path. His clothes are finely made. He peers between the leaves.

The child walks to him. Her head tilts. "Little John, what are you doing?"

The boy yelps and falls on his backside. "What're ya on about? Sneaking up like a sniping marmot. You could kill a man like that!"

The child's lips tilt downward. "I have only seen a sniping marmot in my books."

"Yeah. Well"—he stands and brushes himself off—"L'Hovat's got 'em in droves. Teeth the size of my fingers, they are. And claws just the same. But they're silent as death!"

The child pauses. "So, what are you doing?"

The boy looks to either side before he leans in. "My da and your ma and that scary man are meeting, and I can't go in. I found these yesterday—baby brush swallows! Look!" He pulls back the branches to reveal five baby birds with bright blue eyes, red beaks, and golden feathers.

Her symmetrical eyes widen. The child reaches a hand toward them before pulling back. Her smile is full and toothy. I cannot recall when I last saw her happy. She claps her hands and brushes a small tear from her eye. "Those are beautiful."

"Quite right. Mama says...my mama says it's good luck to see baby brush swallows. They have the power of blessings."

"What blessing do you need?" the child asks as her gaze falls back on the boy.

"To run fast!" the boy says as he sprints around the bush. "To be strong! Look at my muscles. Da says a king needs strong muscles." He pulls back an embroidered sleeve with a sideways smile.

The child steps closer, leaning toward his exposed arm. Her lips purse. "You do need some of those."

The boy pulls down his sleeve. "Oh yeah? Bet I'm still faster than you." He giggles as he taps her shoulder with his fingertips. "You are the Eater. Bet you can't eat me!"

The child looks at her shoulder and then in the direction her tutor went. She smiles, grabs her skirt, and runs after him. The boy is fast, but he slows for her. The child always catches up to him. Her laughter is warm and sweet.

"Kevali. Return to me at once!" The mother's voice screeches through the garden, magicked to be louder.

The child stumbles and falls, skidding hard on the ground. The boy runs back to her. The child has blood on her hands and a hole in her skirt.

She looks behind her, and her eyebrows pinch in the middle. She pushes the boy away. "Run. Run now. She is coming. You can't be seen here with me. Go!"

The boy hesitates. She glares at him. "Run, or even though you are a prince, you will die and never get muscles."

The child rises, and the boy runs. She brushes off the dirt with the back of her hand, twists her skirt to the side, and places her hands behind her back. The boy ducks behind a pine.

Her mother storms toward her. "Kevali, what is the meaning of this? Why did you leave your potions tutor?"

"I came outside to rest."

"There is no rest for a queen, and you will never be a queen without your lessons." The mother twists around, her lips tightly pinched. "What is that sound?"

The child's eyes widen, and she says nothing, though her shoulders tremble. The mother glances at her before stepping up to the bush. "What is this atrocity? Screeching mole rats?"

"Brush swallows." The child clamps her hands to her mouth. The mother raises one eyebrow, then her gaze drops to the child's filthy hands and skirt. The girl whispers. "They bring blessings."

"Brush swallows." The mother's lip curls up. "The only magic here is the magic we control. We do not need the fake blessings of the forest. Be gone!" She clasps an amulet along the chain of her waist, and the chirps are silenced as the bush collapses into a pile of dust and smoke. "We will plant an apple tree here instead. Something with purpose."

The mother strides to the manor house. "And fix yourself up, Kevali. You are as transient and useless as an ephemeral flower until you know your place and learn to maintain your beauty. Remember your purpose. I have great plans for you if you do not ruin them first. The L'Hovat coward is leaving. Get inside now, lest he take you with him."

As the mother slips into the manor, the child looks at the pile of ashes, then falls to her knees. Smoke drifts in swirling forms before her. She scoops up the dust of the bush and holds it close to her chest. A tear strikes the pile in her hand, creating a puff of ash.

"She takes everything from me. Everything I want or love." She sifts a finger through the ash. "I will never forget—never let anyone or anything in. I'll make blessings for myself." Piercing her finger with a thorn, she sets one hand on top of the other, palms together with the ashes in between. With a word, bright light glows from her palms. "But I won't forget you." She closes her eyes. "Birds to apples, dust, and ash. Now sealed in this stone, I'll remember your last."

The child rises. She holds a round obsidian sphere, made with the blood of the birds and the blood of the child, in her palm. She twists her hand again, and in another flash, a silver ring encircles the stone. She holds it up to the light of the sun. "Dark and hard like I will be. I will wear you forever."

She wipes a tear with her scraped and bleeding palm and stands stiffly, her shoulders set, her smile gone. The boy rises slowly, and silently backs away.

As she turns to face me, her cheek is stained with red and black tears.

CHAPTER FIVE

The Queen

Present day

The carriage ride was dull. The people stood silently. Their eyes were lined with dark circles, some reddened and swollen—all as hard as coal. I watched through my fine imported lace. I grimaced at their filth. Yates sat across from me, observing through the other window of the carriage.

"Why do they not greet me? Why do they not cheer for me?"

Yates frowns. "The princess is dead. They are mourning."

I sniffed and brushed something off my dress. "She is." I knew the people might be more somber than me, but this was something else. Something mutinous. I wondered if they would mourn the same way if it had been me.

"Will you hold a funeral, my queen?"

I whirled toward him. "A funeral?" I scoffed.

Yates paled, looking like a wrinkled egg. "Y-yes, my queen. A f-funeral. The people may—"

"The people will forget by supper." And love me instead.

He nodded. "Yes, my queen."

I sat back in my seat, the pores of the lace now blocked by the overlapping fabric. I waved a hand. "Take me home."

Upon our return, I wandered through my castle. The stones were as strong as I was. The floors as cool. The stained glass as perfect. The drapes as clean and elegant. My castle was me, and I was my castle. I twisted the ring on my finger as I stopped by the hallway mirror.

"Mirror, mirror, on the wall, who is the fairest of them all?"

The chorus of voices hummed in my ears and vibrated through my chest. "You are."

I smiled.

Pausing before my glorious portrait, I waited for the sense of pride I had felt when wearing the dress, surrounded by treasures which had shimmered off the canvas as if indwelled by an inner light. But now? I hadn't remembered the gold appearing so lack-luster, or my dress appearing so flat and dull. I frowned and made a mental note to add more lighting around the portrait...and scold Yates for not dusting as well as he should. My magnificence must be radiant.

The general held a meeting as arduous as the last. L'Hovat rebels were raiding at the eastern border. The general wanted to use more aggression to take over their closest cities. Moreover, contention in the trade agreements to the west resulted in Tallen holding our supplies hostage. Worse yet, there was flooding in the southern lowlands and fires across the highlands in the north. They looked to me as if I could fix everything immediately. And, though I was magical, I was not a goddess. I could not change the weather. However, it did seem an obvious solution to take the water from the lowlands and move it to the fire—save them all. Two birds, one stone.

I said as much.

The general nodded, blinking slowly. As if he fought the urge to roll his eyes. "The fires and the floods put our crops at risk for the summer months. We may not have enough food to keep my men fighting."

I peered down at the map, the feeling of being out of my depth creeping coldly across my skin. "Well,"—I pointed to the rebels in L'Hovat—"can we make a new treaty with them?"

He shook his head with an exaggerated sigh. "My queen, that would not work. You know they will not meet with us. Taking from them violently is the only thing that works. We have tried a treaty in the past, but they are hardened—evil."

My eyes flashed to his, and I swept my hair behind my shoulder. We couldn't afford a war right now. If we couldn't feed the army... "Try to treat again."

I watched his eyes close as he clenched his jaw. Angry. I bristled at his insolence.

Yates bowed beside me. I glanced at his wrinkly face.

"My queen, perhaps we can continue to examine our options." He paused until I nodded for him to continue. "Let us readdress these objectives tomorrow." The general and the butler made eye contact before the general bowed and showed himself out.

Yates began to tidy the pastries.

I dragged a finger down the arm of the velvet chair. "The general dislikes my ideas."

Yates hesitated but continued stacking the plates.

"Yates, speak plainly."

"My queen, you are beautiful and wise. You are gifted in magic and trained in the ways of the court." He hesitated. "But, at times, I fear that your extensive training in these things has not provided my queen with other training. Economics. Military strategy. Foreign relations."

Icy fingers wrapped around my heart. "There was no need, of course. The king—"

"Is dead, Your Majesty."

"Yes, I know that."

"And, if I may, his marriageable daughter is now also dead. And so, in our financial situation, we find ourselves—"

I screeched as I stood, clutching my chest. "You think that dead pansy could have fixed this? You know he was going to give her everything!"

Yates dropped the plate to the table with a clatter and bowed low, his fist over his heart. "My queen, forgive me. I did not mean, that is, I—"

"Speak."

"War is not the only way to obtain goods, as you know, my esteemed queen. There are other types of treaties. And...and you are unmarried now."

I dragged my tongue across my teeth as I stared at the tapestry on the wall. My breaths slowed as I understood what he meant. I could remarry. My skin prickled with dread-filled goosebumps. But I was queen. I could pick. I could rule *him*.

My measured breath hissed between my teeth. "And so, I should find a husband...?"

Yates's shoulders visibly relaxed. "Yes, my queen. Ideally, another monarch."

My throat was too dry; perhaps the wine was sour, yet I sipped it desperately.

Marry again. Someone foreign. Someone rich. Someone malleable. My stomach burbled, and lace scratched my skin. Who had tightened my corset so severely? My breaths were unseemly and shallow.

I rose, twisting the ring on my pinky. Suddenly, the room was scorching. I wiped the drops of perspiration from my lip and forehead. "Cool down the fire, Yates. You know better than to roast your queen."

He bowed again with a brow-creased glance to the hearth.

The fireplace was empty.

CHAPTER SIX

The Mirror

Fourteen years earlier

I am the Mirror, and though I can't feel,

I observe and discern all that she reveals.

Though eternal and timeless, yet now, here I rest.

When present to evil, to hush is my test.

The child, now a girl of eighteen, sits before me, her red hair in curls about her shoulders, her dress hangs on a stand behind her. She gets ready in her robe. Today is her wedding. A glittering tiara encircles the top of her head. Her mother observes her with crossed arms as the artist finishes painting her face.

When the artist is finished, the mother grasps the girl's chin. Her eyes narrow and sharpen. "The king will be satisfied."

"Will he now?" The man's voice precedes his entrance into the room, the girl's eyes grow wide, and the mother's shoulders jump in surprise.

"Your Majesty!" the mother says as she gathers herself into a curtsy. The girl stumbles to rise, wraps her robe, and curtsies as well.

The king is dressed in deep violet; gold accents and tassels on his robe glitter in the lamplight. His enormous crown sits on his gray hair, making him six feet tall, but he is otherwise an averagely symmetrical, hard-lined man.

The mother stays low. "What an honor to see you. But—but Majesty, to see the bride before the wedding ceremony—the fates forbid—"

"I care not for the fates," he says with a slash of his hand. "The fates are mine to beckon and mine to control. I am the king. The fates gave me my daughter with your tricks years ago. And now they give me the final piece, the final reward, from our agreement. You've played your part well. Don't flail around now."

His brown eyes rove up and down the girl, and his lips part in a snakelike smile. "Yes. This one shall do. She's trained in magic?"

"She had the best tutors, Your Majesty. Potions, artifacts, spells, mirror magic—"

"She will obey me?"

"She is a servant to the crown, Your Majesty."

"And she will be silent?"

The mother pauses, and the girl shivers. "If you ask it of her."

"I do. Rise." As they stand, he circles the girl. The mother's clasped hands pale from squeezing together. He frowns at the mother. "Leave us."

The mother's lips part. "Your Majesty?"

"I shall not repeat myself."

The mother starts, stops herself from speaking, then turns and leaves. The girl stares straight ahead at the red-papered wall. I, of course, cannot leave, but the king has never spoken to me.

He stops before the girl. "I am your husband and master. I am your king and your lord. You are the gem in my crown. Jewels never speak. They only shine. They go where I place them. Do you understand?"

The girl begins to open her mouth but then simply nods.

"Take off your robe."

She steps back. Her arms clutch the opening tighter. "Your Maj—"

"Silence," he says quietly, but even I hear the threat in those words.

Her hands quake as she stands before him. She spins her obsidian ring and takes a deep breath. Then, with a clench of her eyes, she pulls the tie around her waist, letting the robe flutter to the floor like ash in the garden.

The king walks around her naked form. The girl's jaw is set, and her blue eyes flash open to stare straight ahead. Only I witness the slight brim of tears and recognize the line between her brows as anger.

"You are too thin." The king brushes her spine from her neck to the base with his knuckles.

He presses a finger to her flank. "This mole is unsightly. A queen must be unblemished." In a moment, he pulls at the small, dark tag, and his dagger slices across her skin. He throws the tiny piece of flesh onto the dressing table. The girl cries out but doesn't move. He stands before her, cleaning his dagger on her robe. "Make sure that does not scar. Scars are unacceptable." The girl's fingers clench, constantly twisting the black stone ring. A trail of blood drips down to her waist.

"You are adequate." He pulls in a breath before his fingers drift down from the freckles on her cheeks to her collarbone. "The sun has poisoned your skin here. You may no longer go outside." His fingers tug on a curl of her hair. "At least your hair is lovely. You will be my ruby."

The girl ducks her head with a nod. He grabs her chin. The skin blanches as he holds too tightly. Her hand twitches. The blood drips down to her thigh.

"You are mine, and I shall use you and discard you as I see fit. A jewel that does not shine is discarded. Metal that loses its luster is smelted in the fire. Am I clear?"

A tear trickles down her cheek. Blood drips to the floor.

Three loud knocks sound in the chamber.

"Who disturbs the king?" he asks without turning.

The old butler enters with his eyes on the floor. "Your Majesty, the ceremony is about to begin. The prince of Zafmet demands to sit on the right side. The—"

The king growls. "I am coming." He turns back to the girl. "Clean yourself up. Do not drip on my floor. I will see you at the ceremony." His eyes rove over her body once again. "And after..."

The king leaves, slamming the door.

The girl vomits into the chamber pot.

CHAPTER SEVEN

The Queen

Present day

Another village had been consumed by fire. And three more had been destroyed by flash floods, knocking out the bridge. A delegation from Tallen continued threatening to destroy our supplies if we didn't send more beans, which were trapped on the other side of that bridge. The people threw tomatoes at my carriage when I went out for a ride, their faces lined with hungry, unveiled fury. The funeral pyres of those who died from starvation burned daily. Bags grew under my eyes from sleepless, nightmare-filled nights, because worse yet... I closed my eyes. Worse yet, I had to m—marr—

No. I couldn't do it.

I finally had freedom from the king and could live in opulence. I had killed my greatest rival. I was the most beautiful woman in the world. I had all I'd ever wanted, yet my castle was too big, the halls too empty. No one wanted me as their queen. And my people were dying.

My reflection looked drawn, and deep shadows purpled below my eyes. For the past three weeks I had studied—Yates covered my desk with missives, tomes, and histories—trying to find any other way to finance ourselves out of this crisis. Yates claimed the people could sacrifice no more, and after all the fires and floods, I believed him. The land was unyielding. The weather unceasing in its chaotic destruction. The general pushed for more conflict to steal what we needed at the border, but I resisted. How would I feed an army if I couldn't feed my own city? I had studied and searched and lost sleep looking for another way, any way to unburden myself from having to...remarry.

The fates had turned away from me. The people would never love me. I had no other way to save them.

I sat before my mirror all morning. Staring and not seeing. Speaking these thoughts aloud. The mirror always listened. The mirror had always been there. The mirror had never lied.

A knock at the door announced Yates, his soft three raps as identifiable as his voice. "Your Majesty, forgive me. I have news."

I did not turn, and Yates came to stand behind me. His withered form looked skeletal in the reflection. "You may speak."

He twisted a coil of paper around in his hands, beads of sweat lining his temple. He bowed again. "It is difficult to say this, Your Majesty, but..." He undid his cravat and stuffed it in his pocket.

I frowned at his nervousness.

"Your Majesty, the..." He coughed. "The princess is not dead." He clenched his fist shut, stiffening his shoulders.

My brows tightened for a moment. "The princess...is *not* dead. Is that what you just said?" I asked. Yates nodded. "The princess I poisoned. Snow White." His nodding continued. "How can this be?"

"I'm not sure, Your Highness, but the Thwarven people have placed her in a glass casket, and her form is unchanged. Her lips still moist. Her skin still fresh."

"It's been twenty-eight days."

"Indeed, Your Majesty."

I threw off the shawl and stormed to my mother's spell book. I flipped to the "Sleep of Death" potion and read the ingredients again. "Yates, this is a poison, it will—" My eyes caught on something I had missed before.

Tiny, reversed letters lined the skull at the top of the page. "No." I rushed to grab my hand mirror.

Now correctly oriented in the mirror, they read: "*The sleep like death can be undone with true love's first kiss.*"

"Like? *Like* death? There is an antidote?" I slammed the book shut. "How could I have missed this? How—" I paused, and for the first time in weeks, a flicker of light, suspiciously like hope, began to break through. "An antidote," I whispered greedily.

I turned to Yates who stepped back cautiously, his eyes wide and his brow furrowed. "Yates. We can save the kingdom."

All his wrinkles crinkled into a frown. "Your Majesty?"

"We will wake the princess. She will marry. Her new husband will support our kingdom. I can remain queen!"

"But who loves the princess? Who would kiss her?"

"Not I, of course, but someone must." I pointed between Yates and me. "We will find her a prince. She will go to his castle and rule there. I will never have to see her again!"

"Majesty, I hesitate to say this, but you will no longer be the fairest in the land."

I paused my pacing and glanced toward the mirror. "Perhaps I can scar her face first." I waved off the thought. "No matter. She will be in another kingdom." I twisted and paced toward Yates. "Who are the eligible princes? Tallen has a four-year-old. Gotsburg's prince is sixty-five."

"One of the Zafmet princes might work, Your Majesty. Prince Damian is forty-two, Prince Caiden is twenty-one, and Zafmet has expressed a desire to renegotiate trade terms."

"Yates, you're a genius," I exclaimed, making the poor skeleton jump. "Bring the delegation to the throne room. We need to bring Prince Damian to the castle immediately. He will wed her and whisk her away. And then I can rule in peace."

With a bow, Yates left the room. His footsteps echoed down the hall.

Silence reigned, and I crossed my arms as I stared at the mirror before me. I had never looked at it with suspicion, but doubt flooded my chest. "Mirror, mirror on the wall, did you know the princess lived?"

The thousand voices rolled and rumbled before it answered, "I did."

"Why did you not say so? You said that she—"

"She no longer breathed."

"Why would you not tell me?"

"You did not ask the right question."

I did not ask specifically if she lived. The mirror never lied, but I never expected that the mirror might withhold information. That the mirror... But it was objective. Unbiased. True. Still... if the truth was mutable by the method of a question, what did that mean?

"You're right, Mirror. Am I still the fairest of them all?"

"You are but—" The voices cut off sharply.

"Mirror, what were you going to say?"

The mirror held its reflective tongue. I grabbed my shawl and nearly fled from the room. If I didn't have the mirror, then I was truly alone. I scoffed as I stormed out. I was done talking with inanimate objects. I had a plan that could save us all.

It was time to raise a dead girl.

Chapter Eight

The Mirror

Ten years earlier

I am the Mirror, no more or no less.

Enchanted and ageless, I reflect and assess.

When others are present, there's one facet I see,

Yet when she's alone, she shows her true self to me.

The queen places pearl-tipped barrettes throughout her red hair; each shines like the stars at sunset. A giggle bursts from under the queen's bed.

She turns. "Snow White?"

There is silence, then another giggle.

The queen turns back to face me. "Come out now. Princesses do not snicker under bedsheets. And eight is too old to hide."

"Aw, but Mama Kiva, I love to hide!" The little girl emerges and brushes dust from her velvet gown before sitting down in front of the queen. "I'm good at it too. Bet you didn't even know I was here."

The queen reaches for her brush and begins to untangle the princess's long black hair. Her elegant fingers pluck out a green leaf. "Who are you hiding from?"

The girl fiddles with a barrette she took from the table. "Some boys."

The queen frowns slightly before grabbing some pins to form a rose-shaped bun with the top half of her hair. "I see."

"Can I have pearls like you?" The queen nods and tucks them in. "Look! We are twins now! We are so pretty."

The queen's lips lift at the sides, a rare sight. "We are pretty. You are a beautiful girl."

"Yes. And did you see my pictures? I'm a really good drawler." The queen's hands pause as she puffs blush on the girl's cheeks, but the princess continues. "You don't ever drawl, so you must be bad."

The queen selects clear shine for the princess's red lips. "I painted when I was younger."

"Are you very old now?"

"Not very."

"Can I see your drawlings?" Her eyes widen.

The queen smiles. "No."

"Can I show you mine?" The girl bounces up and down in her seat. "Today, I drawled a fat cat."

The queen laughs quietly, a pretty sound I hadn't heard recently. "I would like to see your fat cat." She finishes a coal lining along the princess's lashes before declaring. "Finished."

The princess leans toward me and admires her reflection. "I look so pretty. I'm glad I have you." The princess reaches for the queen.

The queen squeezes her small hand. "And I—"

The king bellows as he enters the room, slamming the door behind him. "Where is my daughter, Kevali? What have you done with her?" The queen flinches, then her face turns as flat as my glass. The king stops and smiles at the princess. His voice is softer now. "Snow, where have you been?"

The princess rises and walks to her father, who pats her head, clutching some strands between his fingers. "Mama K—I mean, the queen—did my hair."

"And you are the loveliest in all the land! Look at your hair! Like the constellations!" The king has moved to stand behind the queen and presses the princess beside her. The king looks between the two before him. "It is decided that black hair is most beautiful. Though your hair is fine, Kevali, it is not as rich as this." He threads his fingers through the princess's locks.

The queen bobs her head, her eyes fixed on the table.

The king then reaches for the queen's hair, his lip curling. "And so, you shall wear your hair up. Put it away."

The queen blinks once, then twice. "Put my hair up, my king?"

"Hat, hood, I care not. Your hair is mine. I will not allow it to compete with Snow's. In the castle and in the sight of others, you will cover it." The queen reaches for a lock of hair at his hard words, her brows pinched.

He spins the princess toward him. "And this child will shine above all others. The fairest in all the lands. You will marry an emperor and shower his wealth on me and our people. I will guide him and help you rule forever!"

The princess smiles, but she casts a look toward the queen.

"Come, my princess. Let's get you back to your lessons."

The princess makes it to the door before turning around and running back to hug the queen. "Thank you for making me pretty. I love you." Then the princess runs from the room, her hair trailing behind her in obsidian waves.

The door clicks shut. Tears well up in the queen's eyelids, though she shows nothing else on her face. Her eyes look deadened. Holding a mass of red hair in one trembling hand, she slowly rolls the strands between her fingertips. "I have given him everything. Still, he asks for more. Only more." A tear trails down her face. "Hat, hood," she says mockingly. "Put it up. It is mine."

With a slow breath, her hands still. "I would cut it all off, but he will kill me. He will beat me. He will use me. He will hurt me." The queen's face falls into her hands. "I am fairest. I am beautiful. I am queen." She rocks back and forth. "I am alone. I am alone. I am alone."

Time passes. The queen shifts, and her voice crackles. "Mirror?"

"Yes, my queen?"

"Am I the fairest?"

"Yes, though the princess grows in beauty."

"Will she be fairer than me?"

"I cannot say, my queen. I can only speak what I see."

"What should I do?"

"My queen?"

"Who am I if not the fairest of them all?"

I say only what I know. "You are the queen. You are beautiful."

"But is that enough?"

There are no answers to that question that I could see, so I say nothing.

CHAPTER NINE

The Queen

Present day

The room was full, the guests comfortably seated, and I was decorated to perfection as I arrived to the feast for the princes of Zafmet. Tomorrow, they would journey to wake the princess.

Yates announced my arrival, and the room hushed. A prince had been seated on either side of my chair; their men filled in the rest of the table. I sat at the head of the feast. The princes were finely dressed, their gently curling black hair nearly as deep a shade as Snow's but with light chestnut, almost olive-toned, skin. Their eyes were a startling light green-blue, bright against the darker hues of their other features. The elder prince had dark scruff along his jaw and a lined forehead, while the younger looked more like a child.

It had been hard enough to convince the diplomats of the plan two weeks ago; now, I could see the princes' thinly veiled skepticism.

Yates pulled my chair back. I stood and cast my hands out to the side, palms up. "Our fair nation welcomes the finest men of Zafmet. To honor our peace and to foster the future, we hold this feast in your honor to thank you and welcome you to Acacia." I lifted my hands, and the room rose with me. "And now if you will join me in a moment of silence for the princess, who cannot yet be here, as we pray for her rapid return with her true love." All the men bowed their heads, including my knights and the staff. I caught Yates's eye and ducked my own head. Ice flooded through my veins with panic. How long was I supposed to stand here? After a few moments, Yates's shoe tapped twice on my chair.

I looked up, grateful for the cue, and raised my glass. "Thank you. To peace, unity and"—I cleared my throat—"love!" The men raised their glasses, and we drank. "Please enjoy your fill."

I sat and reveled in Yates's smile, annoyed at myself for being pleased by his approval. I was queen. I didn't need anyone's approval. But, despite my many years as a royal, I had never been treated as anything more than a walking piece of jewelry. As lovely as I was, my voice ached to be used, my mind eager to be applied. Yet, actually leading felt so very different than watching the king lead. Yates's encouragement made me feel a different kind of pride.

"Your Majesty, the food is wonderful," the baby-faced Prince Caiden said with his fingers ripping into a hot roll. The bones of the quail were already stripped bare on his plate next to the three potato dishes.

The table was brimming with food that I had acquired to show Acacia's strength and value to the princes. A niggling worry itched at my mind as I remembered the hunger of my people but if I could secure this agreement, then all would be fed. "I am glad it is to your liking. Is it very similar to your own seasonings at home?"

The young prince flew into a flurry of details—something called curry, and a flat bread... Though I tried to engage, I couldn't help but think about the princes' trip. The Thwarven lands were to the west, in a forest that was near the mines of the lower hills of the Spires. From what the general had said, the L'Hovat raiders were reported to be just south of there. My chair thumped as Yates gave it a tap. I looked up at him, then over to the princes. I had missed something.

"Yes?"

Prince Damian leaned forward. "Forgive my impertinence, Your Majesty, but if the princess is alive, why have you not brought her to the castle?"

I swallowed, then shifted the linen on my lap. "Given the nature of the curse, we did not wish to move the princess and risk her succumbing to the poison. Our tomes suggest that only true love's kiss can save her but say nothing about what might cause her actual death." And I hadn't wanted to see her, but I did not say that aloud.

Caiden rubbed at his bare chin. His youthfulness reminded me of her. "Your Majesty, how can Damian fall in love with the princess if he doesn't know her?"

My brows furrowed. "She is beautiful."

The princes both pinched their lips. Damian looked like he was ready to speak, ready to withdraw and go home. Ready to refuse. A plan formed hastily in my mind.

"And—and her...friend...will be accompanying you to tell you about her, so your judgments and affections may be complete." I froze, wondering how I would explain Snow White's confusion when she woke, but relaxed as the tension in their shoulders softened at my words. I would think of something brilliant by then.

They shared a long glance together before Damian nodded. "Then we will do what we can. If we are successful, we will return to complete the trade agreement. If unsuccessful, we will leave in peace."

I nodded, relieved. My mind raced through the potion I would need to concoct later that evening. "I thank you for your courage and willingness."

Caiden reached for a puffed pastry. "I am excited to be here. Though we are generally well-traveled, I've never been to Acacia before. I heard that there may be magic here." I froze, midway through my asparagus spear. Caiden continued, "We have our own wise ones and jesters, but not *real* magic. I thought that had left with the elves and fairies and those massive ancient creatures."

"Elves and fairies, brother? Really?" Damian chuckled, casting me an apologetic look. "I think you've spent more times with fairytales than history books."

"Better than stuck in meetings and drowning in economics like you."

Damian raised a brow. "You'll need those, too, one day, in case I die of the plague."

Caiden laughed aloud. "Fear not, brother, I have brought a few especially boring books to help me get to sleep on our journey. I will return well-educated from this venture." He turned back to me. Their interactions were so...warm. "But, Your Majesty, is there really magic here?" He leaned in, his light eyes glittering in the candlelight.

I dabbed my lips with a napkin before setting it back on my lap, swallowing. "Of course, Prince Caiden. There are a few here who can use magic. Although, not as many as in years past."

"Amazing," Caiden said. "Can I meet one?"

"Isn't magic dangerous?" Damian asked over his brother.

I glanced down to the sword at his hip. "Is your sword dangerous?"

His hand automatically went to the hilt. My knights stiffened. "It is when I wield it. But it is only a tool."

I met his gaze and nodded. "Just so."

The brothers fell into easy conversation with those beside them, and I let out a breath. I tried not to think about the ways my magic had deceived and harmed others or how it must deceive them all again tomorrow. Magic could be dangerous. I could be dangerous. But I, I mean, magic, was only a tool.

I excused myself early, claiming a headache, and hurried to my chambers. It had taken years for me to decide to send the huntsman after Snow, then more time to decide to poison her myself. The irony that I would be transforming again—only this time to save, not harm, the princess—was not lost on me. This potion would change me into a dull and unimpressive dishwater blonde with average, younger features. It was the perfect disguise, but so common. I shuddered at the thought of my magic being suppressed while under the disguise, but at least it would be temporary. At least, the mirror would still know my true beauty.

I had to prepare. I had mere days to convince Prince Damian to love her, revive her, and wed her. I could not fail again.

CHAPTER TEN

The Mirror

Five years earlier

I am the Mirror, but no source of light.

Shadows and brightness reflect in my might.

But although I show things just as I see,

I can't help but wonder if the problem is me.

The debutante ball is full. Young men and women have come from across the country, arrayed in their finest. The women's dresses are large, and their jewelry glitters from the thousands of candles above them. I line the walls, reflecting all the glory and wonder. Several dancers catch an image of themselves and correct a cravat or calm a wayward hair. I reflect the truth.

The queen arrives first. Unaccompanied. The doors open, the music halts, and the dancers step aside as she walks to her throne above the dance floor. Her dress is violet, and a smooth black coif covers her hair and frames her face before clinging tightly to her neck and chest. Her crown sits atop the coif. Her eyes are distant, but symmetrical and lovely. She sits alone.

The trumpets sound. "Presenting His Royal Highness King Rorin. And presenting for her debut, Her Royal Highness Princess Snow White!" The princess wears white tulle, her dress finer than all the others. Pearl barrettes line her hair, and gemstones glitter from every aspect of her gown. Every move makes her shimmer with light.

The king leads the princess to the center, while the queen's piercing gaze follows the princess. Their relationship is as strained today as it has been for the last two years. The king speaks. "Thank you all for joining me as we celebrate the thirteenth birthday of my beautiful daughter, Snow White. Lovelier and more fair than any diamond, you outshine them all."

The music starts again, and the two dance their waltz, soon joined—at the director's cue—by the rest of the room. Laughing and pink-cheeked, the princess is never at a loss for partners. The king socializes with his noble families, the general, and the women of his court, always with a drink in his hand.

The queen remains seated on her throne.

The room pauses when a woman arrives. Her hair is black and wavy and falls past her hips. Her dark eyes need no kohl. The king sees her and walks toward her with welcoming arms. After guiding her across the room, he leads her up the steps toward the thrones.

The queen frowns. The princess dashes up the steps and grabs the king's other arm, begging him to come dance with her again. He smiles at her with glassy eyes that quickly return to the woman from the Isle. The king glances toward the queen.

"Kevali, you have no drink. Won't you partake?"

The queen shakes her head and stares at the woman who slowly licks the bottom of her lips. The king watches her movement like a hound watches a rabbit.

His voice is hoarse. "Kevali, rise. Our visitor needs a rest."

The queen's shoulders stiffen. "My king?"

"Our esteemed guest requires rest."

The queen glances toward the benches, chairs, and couches by the fire. "Then let her rest."

The king growls, then sits and pulls the woman onto his lap. She laughs and clings to the lapels of his coat. Whispers flutter across the room. The queen looks wide-eyed, then blinks her expression clear again. She stares ahead.

The king's lip pulls up at the side. "See, Kevali. The lady rests."

The queen does not reply. The princess's face flashes with pain as she looks upon the queen, then dashes back down the stairs. She hasn't spoken to the queen since That Day and does not start today. And then, she appears distracted back to happiness when she is begged to join a new dance.

The king murmurs to the woman who lets out a high, tittering laugh. "My lady, you have such fine hair. So dark and rich."

The butler comes and whispers something into the king's ear. His face turns red. He whispers something back, spittle flying between the words. The butler retreats with a deeply lined face and resumes his place by the queen. The king tucks his face into the woman's neck.

The queen spins her obsidian ring before she rises. "Alas, I must retire."

The king snorts. "So soon, Kevali?" His teeth show as his lip curls up. He tugs the woman farther onto his lap as the queen descends, surrounded by hushed words that seem to crescendo as she takes her leave.

In her private hall, the queen throws her crown, then rips off her hair cover to cast it to the floor. Her long red curls fall around her, and the butler chases each piece she casts aside.

She storms like a tempest. "Yates. How—" She starts and stops. "This is too far. In front of—*everyone*!" She pulls at her hair as she flies back down the hall.

Yates skips to keep up. "I tried, Your Majesty. I believe the king has had too much to drink."

"How many, Yates?" she asks. The butler pulls up short, his face tightly drawn. The queen rounds on him and stands very still. "How. Many. Others? Do not lie to me as if she is the first."

His cheeks turn a dark burgundy. "They began arriving eight months ago. I am sorry, Your Majesty. I do not know the number."

The queen hisses. "Hedonist." She whirls her manicured hand and knocks a vase to the ground. "But in front of the whole kingdom? Making a mockery out of me. It was already too much to release that *child* into society! At thirteen, Yates!" A shudder shakes through her before she turns to the butler. "Thank you for the truth. You are dismissed."

"Your Majesty?"

"Leave me, Yates. Just go."

He pauses for a moment before saying quietly, "I am sorry, Your Majesty."

The queen takes a deep breath before she turns to me, fiery wall sconces beside me. Her eyes are wild, her lips bared in a snarl. She clings to my side columns. Her voice is a whisper, harsh and uneven. "Mirror, mirror, on the wall, who is the fairest of them all?"

"Famed is your beauty, Majesty, but yet, I see a lovely maid. Tulle cannot hide her gentle grace. Alas, she is fairer than you are."

"Alas for *her*!" The queen throws her earrings to the ground. "Who is she?"

"Her lips are red as a blood, her hair black as obsidian, and her skin white as pearl."

She clutches at her throat. "Snow White?" The queen huffs a breath. "So, the time has finally come. That treacherous princess usurps everything I have worked for. Every torture I have endured to be queen, to be lovely, to be wanted. Damn them. Damn them all!" Her skin pales and moistens. "Mother said it would be enough!"

The queen collapses to the floor, and her cries echo down the hall.

CHAPTER ELEVEN

The Queen

Present day

Although I pushed my cheek and twisted my nose, it still didn't seem like the face I wore belonged to me. My hair, now a nasty muddy-straw color, fell just past my shoulders. My eyes were a darkened peat moss, so different from their typical blue. In a last-minute spray of magic, I'd added freckles. Anything to set my face back a decade.

I poked the dots on my face. I'd had freckles once. But after so many years away from the sun, protected by the king, they had faded out. What would my face look like now if I dared expose it to the sun again?

For today, the disguise was set, and though the twice-daily potion tasted somewhere between sour milk and decaying mouse, it would be worth it. The journey could take as long as seven days, so I had prepared enough of the potion to last a month. I packed most of it in the large traveler's bag but carried six little glass vials in my waist purse.

Part of me was terrified to be doing this.

The other part of me, now unleashed from the shackles of the dead and rotting king, unweighted by a crown, and hidden from anyone who might recognize me, was scandalously giddy. I almost laughed at the impropriety of traveling with a group of men. Sleeping in tents and—I blinked hard—I would have to use the toilet *outside*.

No matter. Commoners and cows did it. Surely, I could manage.

I would have to maintain this visage and hide my true self, but I had been molded by my mother and the king into the perfect actress, with a heart and face of impassive clay. Surely this was another outlandish form of acting.

Yates entered quietly and stood by the door as I prepared my final items in a guest room. I pointedly ignored his crossed arms and dark scowl. He usually wasn't so forthcoming with his displeasure.

"You cannot talk me out of this, Yates."

"Please, Your Majesty, rethink this plan. You, alone, with these—these *rogues* and *ruffians,* is absolutely, positively—"

"What I plan to do." I turned to him, mischief peaking my brow. "Rogues and ruffians? Yates, the princes, and their personal guard are not—"

"With all due respect, you do not know. You have no experience."

I pointed directly at him. "Precisely." I walked toward the hook and grabbed my heavy cloak. "I have no experience. You've said as much before. The general knows it. The people know it. I am floundering, Yates, *floundering* in ruling my kingdom because I have no experience. I am not stupid. I have worked to improve, but it isn't enough."

He opened his mouth to argue, but I held up my hand. "You have been my one true ally throughout this whole cursed existence of mine. The one person I trust, besides my mirror and my magic. And, frankly, those have failed me." The mirror on the wall rattled slightly on its nail.

"Your Majesty, this is exactly why I cannot let you go."

"Yates." I grabbed his old, wrinkled hand, rolling my fingers over the soft rolls of paper-thin skin. "This is exactly why you must. You have watched me exist, not live, *dying* a little more each day I spend within these castle walls. Now, I have a chance to save this kingdom—my kingdom—and maybe even witness the needs of my people. And if I can acquire funds for our nation through this marriage, we need not be overrun by L'Hovat nor be so easily threatened by Tallen. The people might even love me if they had food in their bellies. I need to do this."

"Your Majesty..." His eyes were pleading, begging, and his grip tightened on mine.

"You'll be fine." As I regarded his face, something stirred in my chest, warm and unexpected. "Oh, Yates, I'm coming back."

He set his hand on my shoulder in a moment of impulse before drawing it back a moment later. "You'd best. Forgive my forwardness, but you're the closest thing I've had to a daughter, and I'm not willing to lose you." He stepped back, then bowed low and set out for the main entrance. I stood, stunned into silence as I stared after him. Like a daughter? Shaking my head, I rushed behind him as he approached the princes and their retinue out by the horses.

Yates bowed. "Your Royal Highnesses, I would like to present Lady Val. She was a lady-in-waiting and friend to the princess. She has been asked to provide you with any information you wish to know about Princess Snow."

The two princes looked me over and dipped their heads in a slight bow.

"We are pleased to meet you. Thank you for accompanying us." Damian glanced behind him and scratched the back of his hand. "I'm afraid it will be rough travel, though, my lady."

I stepped forward with a plastered smile. My cheeks ached to hold it after years of disuse. "It is my"—Yates quickly tugged on my sleeve, and I fell into the deep curtsy I had forgotten to perform, my knees groaning—"great honor to travel with you all, no matter the circumstances."

"I'm sorry the queen couldn't be here to see you go. She is unwell today," Yates added.

Damian and Caiden shared a look before Damian turned to his men and pointed toward the door. The men fell into step immediately and marched out. My lips tipped downward at the group's rapid response.

I doubted I could do that with my own knights. Not without mortal threats.

Damian tipped his head to Yates. "We will do our best to return with the princess. Give the queen our wishes for a rapid recovery." The princes followed the men out.

Yates touched my elbow and leaned in, his eyes full of worry. "Please be careful."

My smile stayed in place, this time, from an inner energy. Nearly vibrating with all the energy and mixed emotions of what I was about to do, I winked. His surprised brows were worth the gesture. I fell into line behind the princes and approached the rows of stomping beasts.

Like every lady, I had learned to ride. But I had also been kept a near prisoner for fifteen years. Somehow the mare seemed more massive and menacing than I remembered...and much more bear than equine. She turned her head and snorted at me loudly with a stomp of her massive hind leg. Embarrassingly, I squeaked and leapt back.

I did not know how to threaten a horse to comply to docility.

Caiden arrived quickly at my side and took the reins from the stable boy with a smile. "My lady, do you not ride?"

"I have... Before. A while ago."

"May I?" The boy prince knelt and offered his hands for me to step into. I froze, looking into his light green eyes for the deceit, betrayal, or cruelty I had come to expect, but there was none.

"Okay..." I started to step into his hand when large hands gripped my waist and set me upon the mare in an instant. I'd like to say I did not yelp, but I would be lying. My heart thundered from the terror of being grabbed; although I knew the king was dead, my face still froze with a sheen of cold sweat.

"Apologies, my lady. Caiden can help next time. We need to move out. Hold tight. Squeeze your knees so you don't fall." Damian continued talking as he tucked my feet into the stirrups and tightened the leather straps. He paused with a frown as he took in my expression for the first time, glancing at his brother and then back to me. "My lady?"

"I'm alright." I breathed.

He studied me further, then nodded to his brother. "Caiden. Mount up."

The young prince was somehow uncowed by the direct language but mock saluted his brother before sauntering to his horse. "Next time, my lady."

Damian rolled his eyes at his brother, before glancing at me one last time and mounting his massive steed.

"Men, line up. Caiden, you're in the fifth row. The lady will be in the third. Hold the line!" Damian called as he ran his horse back and forth along the troop. Soldiers came alongside my own horse. The men and horses eagerly shifted around me. The energy of the group surged until it felt ready to burst. "Ready in the rear?" he called.

"Aye!"

"Out we go. Lead ho!"

A horn sounded and the front of the group shot out from the keep in a full gallop. My horse stomped and beat the ground, ready and chomping at the bit. When the horses before us lurched forward, she took off with a screeching whinny. I held tightly to the leather reins and leaned forward, my legs slipping backward down her flanks.

I was terrified.

I was exhilarated.

Surrounded before and behind and beside by soldiers, we raced out of the town. The dirt-blonde hair I'd adopted fluttered behind me. The princes were making some sort of statement—a loud and wild one. A lightness buoyed up from my chest, and I felt dangerous and free and a part of something thunderous. A real smile broke upon my lips.

Finally, out of sight of the hamlet, the older prince called for a halt. The horses heaved massive breaths, their chests shifting several inches in every exhale, yet they still twitched and stamped as if they could run forever.

"Scout team, ahead! Tail, hold for two." The men divided into groups, and four took off down the road.

The rest of us moved forward at a walk. Though the dust tickled my lungs, I couldn't remember the last time I'd felt the fresh, cutting wind like this. I turned my face to the blinding sun to feel its warmth.

"The lady seems pleased," Caiden said as he sped up to ride beside me.

I shifted in my seat, uncertain how a lady-in-waiting would act with a prince. "I am."

Damian joined us on his mount. "I'm glad that you were able to hold on," he said with a smirk. "That is the way of the Zafmet guard, but I was afraid I'd have to return for you and pick you up off the ground."

"You could have chosen a gentle gallop, brother." Caiden laughed. "It would be awkward to trample the lady just outside the keep."

I gaped at them. Just awkward? My defenses rose until I realized they were joking with me.

Caiden winked as Damian cleared his throat. "Alright, my lady. We have at least three days to ride to the forest and two by foot to reach the shrine the dwarves—"

"Thwarven," I say. "They are no more dwarves than I'm an elf."

Damian paused with a glance to his brother before he continued. "Thwarven, then. While we travel, tell us about the princess."

I swallowed and strained to think of positive qualities. "Well. She is the"—I pressed the words out through my teeth—"fairest maiden in all the land. Her father designed her with the use of magic." My mother's magic. "Her lips are red as a blood, her hair black as obsidian, and her skin white as pearl."

Damian, whose eyes had widened at the mention of magic, blinked through the surprise. "And, what else?" Damian focused on the horizon. Mission-driven.

"Ah." What else was there to say? "Her...hair falls to her waist, and she often adorns it with pearls like stars in the night. Her form is pleasing, and her height is a few inches below mine. She was presented to the court at thirteen—"

"Thirteen!" Caiden exclaimed. "So young? We must be sixteen in Zafmet."

"Yes, thirteen. Her father wished her to be well matched."

The creases of Damian's brow deepened. "If she was presented so early, why had she not been betrothed? I do not remember my father mentioning any potential marriage alliances before your queen's recent contact."

My fingers pulled at the reins in my hand, picking at a string that had loosened on one side. "Ah, well. He died. But before that, the king was focused on local matches. He enjoyed dangling the princess like bait to keep the nobles in line for years as they waited for a betrothal."

Both princes stiffened. The words I had just uttered were slanderous and...treasonous.

I backpedaled. "Ah, that is to say, the king—I'm sorry, that was impertinent—the king wanted the absolute best match for Snow White and had...had not yet been satisfied." I swallowed through a lump of discomfort, my tongue as dry as ash. Apparently, while I had years of practice in staying silent, I was not practiced at filtered and flowery speech. Now unleashed, my tongue was sharp and direct.

Caiden started to speak, but Damian spoke first. "Well, every father wants what's best for his daughter."

I nodded, my cheeks still warm.

"Please continue."

I slowly inhaled, cursing my reckless decision to come along. What more could they want to know? "Her feet are petite. She looks best in colors like gemstones, but she prefers blues, yellows...ruby." The princes were silent again. I cleared my throat. "So that's her, Your Highnesses."

"While I appreciate all that you have shared, I do wish you to tell us more about her."

"What more do you want to know? She is the pinnacle of beauty."

"Yes, but what else?"

I couldn't stop the harsh laugh that came out. "What else? Do you want to hear how she would give her own jewelry to beggars in the street? How she ruined dresses when she helped the kitchen maids? Those actions did nothing but dim her beauty. What matters more than beauty?"

Damian cast a glance at his brother, and discomfort once again wiggled in my chest.

"Everything matters more than beauty, my lady. Everything."

It was my turn to frown. Maybe these princes were daft after all.

CHAPTER TWELVE

The Mirror

Present day

I am the Mirror, and though small in her hand,

I can hear and can see as she travels the land.

My queen, yet disguised, shows her character true.

For the first time, I wonder if we can change with the view.

CHAPTER THIRTEEN

The Queen

Present day

After several hours on horseback—and a notable blister was developing on my ankle in addition to the bruising on my thighs—I once again wondered if I had been too hasty to try to kill the princess.

It was the perfect plan, brewed from years of pain, and if my daft husband had not attempted to control me from the grave, perhaps she could have lived. But he had wanted to give the princess my crown. My crown! To give it up, pass it over, step back to dowager queen, and let that apple-cheeked toddler run the kingdom and cage me from the grave. No. I would not then nor ever give that power to someone who would find new ways to control me. Especially now that freedom was finally mine. Not now that he was dead. And not to that treacherous child.

How often I had dreamed of deliberately killing him. Dreamed of his terror, as his eyes met mine, knowing that I had been the cause of his death and feeling Justice. But no. Though I had indirectly contributed to his death, the king had died, instead, from a drunken night of debauchery, inhaling his own vomit, and dying in a hot, feverish, coughing mess days later. As he lay in the sick bed, surrounded by the magicians and physicians, he called for my hair before he wheezed his last. Not me. My hair. To threaten me one last time.

Good riddance to the wretched king.

Good riddance to his perfect daughter.

The sooner Prince Damian and the princess kissed and went back to his kingdom, the better.

Finally, we turned off the road and headed deep within a copse of deciduous trees.

My forehead furrowed. "We are stopping for a meal?"

Caiden smiled. "No, for the night."

I tilted my head, glancing briefly to the sky. "But the sun is still up."

"Yes, my lady, but the camp takes time to set up, and food takes time to prepare."

"We will go as fast as we are able," Damian said as he approached the wooden stand, sliding off and tying his mount. He turned to me. "Care for your horse, then report to the blue tent. Caiden, watch those in B group, please. They've been dragging today." As he turned away, I struggled to get off my saddle, straightening and sliding my stiff and aching knee around the top of the horse. Before I knew it, my foot slipped and fell through the stirrup, throwing my body toward the ground.

My arm wrenched back as I was caught by none other than Prince Damian himself. My cheeks burned almost as much as my shoulder.

"Caiden, her foot," Damian said.

He held me, suspended between him and the horse as Caiden struggled and failed to release my ankle from within the stirrup.

"Twist and point the foot, Caiden," Damian commanded. My horse stepped away, pulling me tauter.

"I'm trying. It's this cursed boot."

"Do NOT remove my boot, sir." I squeaked, unwilling to have any male so close to my feet after riding in the sun. "Put me down or lift me back up. I'll get it myself."

Caiden pulled some more and jerked the wood against my ankle bones.

"Ow."

"I'm done with this," Caiden said with a hiss as he reached beneath the horse.

"Wait! Don't—" Damian started, but Caiden had already released the strap under the belly, and the whole saddle fell off, landing on the ground in a cloud of dust. The force yanked me down with Damian, who had been tipped off balance by the sudden lurch. We tumbled to the earth together in a tangle of limbs.

"Oh, Prince Damian, I—" I attempt to untwist one of my arms that had somehow become pinned beneath him. He looked as red-faced as I felt.

"Damian, I'm sorry. I thought—" Caiden started.

"Just grab the good lady, please." As Caiden lifted, Damian rose and helped pull me to my feet.

With the saddle now on the ground, I bent and pointed my toe, slipping my heel back through the stirrup before I straightened to brush my dress off.

Caiden looked like a kicked puppy. He wrung his hands, as if looking for some way to undo it all. "Lady Val, I apologize. I did not mean to release the saddle and drop you. Are you alright?"

"I am. Honestly. If I had been able to dismount skillfully, none of us would be here." I was sure my cheeks shone as red as that poisoned apple. "I lack experience." The words slipped out bitterly.

Damian, the saddle already in his hands, stood behind Caiden and glared at a group of men who failed to conceal their laughter. At me. My spine stiffened. I would not be mocked.

"We all lack experience until we gain it. Next time, I'm confident it will go differently." Damian said, his voice interrupting my anger. "Caiden, would you guide her through the brushing, then point her toward the blue tent? I need to talk with them." His head angled toward the men, who bustled to gather their things. Caiden nodded, his shoulders straight with his new duty.

Grabbing the saddle from Damian, Caiden pulled a stiff brush from the saddlebag and ran through the steps of caring for a horse.

After observing me for a moment, Caiden asked, "The princess doesn't ride?"

"The princess rides quite well, I understand." I had seen her from my room. "The king ensured that she had the best trainers, and she was allowed outside as long as she stayed under many sun coverings." I grimaced at the filth that caked my fingertips. Deep breath. I could do this.

"But you were not?"

My eyes widened, and I froze. "Oh. I...had other duties."

Bless him. Though he clearly had more questions, he did not press me for further explanations.

After we finished, Caiden pointed me to a blue tent. "Wash up with those," he said, indicating the dusty black waterskin, "then head inside. Chef will show you what to do."

"Chef? I am to cook?"

"Tonight is a training night for the men, so yes, tonight, you'll help prepare the meal."

Bitterness boiled in my chest. "Is this because I'm the only female in the group?"

Damian appeared beside us and began washing his hands as well. "Each group takes a shift. Caiden is on tomorrow. I, the next day."

My indignation deflated. "Oh."

"The group only functions as one unit. We all serve each other."

Lifting my eyes, I met Damian's gaze. He couldn't be serious. "But you are princes."

"Princes, kings, queens—we are the ultimate servants of the people. We get the privilege of making hard decisions on behalf of all the people, but how can we make such decisions without first knowing, serving, and earning the trust of those we make decisions for?"

I had no answer. His sentiment, though impractical and naïve, struck something deep and aching inside me. I shoved the feeling down. "I don't know how to cook."

"Neither does Caiden."

"Hey!" Caiden laughed. "I'm not as bad as Chaddeus!"

The brothers chuckled as a large man, covered in stains and flour, burst from the food tent, and added, "I was cleaning up his mess for three days."

"Lady Val, Chef. Chef, Lady Val." Damian introduced us with a wave of his hand.

"Lady V, come on in. Tonight, we feast! The queen's kitchen gave us fresh lambs to roast. We shall not waste such a treat!" I shuffled uncomfortably as I thought of the farmers I had obtained those lambs from to feed the Zafmet party. It was only a few lambs, so why did Chef seem so pleased? Before I could settle on an answer, Chef had stuffed my hands with sticks that smelled like pine along with three fistfuls of tiny smelly leaves. "Here. You can make the rub."

When Damian pressed his hand on the small of my back, guiding me toward the tent, I couldn't prevent myself from flinching. I had not prepared to be touched.

Ducking into the tent, I followed the bustling giant through the packed space. "Use this to crush everything in this bowl into a thick slurry." He passed me a mortar and pestle before sloshing pressed oil into the bottom. He turned back to the flour.

Setting the sticks down beside my armful of greens, I looked between them, then the bowl. At least my herbalism and potion making had prepared me for this. I eyed the suddenly very large pile of herbs beside me.

"How shall I finish that in time?" I asked as I pulled out another sprig.

"One at a time, lass. Just one at a time."

My hands quaked, and my back burned from the effort of crushing leaves, but I did it. Every stinking leaf from every single stem. I stared at the pile. It was much larger than any I had worked with before. I started pushing, spinning, and pulling before finally lifting the rock stick like a bludgeon and beating the leaves.

"Lass, lass, what are you doing?" Chef hollered as he rushed over. "You're cooking, not beating!" He chuckled and added a bit more oil and salt crystals. "Just a bit softer, lass. If you need to release some energy, I'm sure there is a practice sword you could swing around later." His laughter pulled a smile to my lips, and I finished transforming the massive bowl into a slurry. I sat back, satisfied.

"Well done, lass. Now rub that all over the lamb." Without warning, he threw a skinned, bloody lamb on the table in front of me.

I yelped as I eyed the distorted creature. "I need to touch that?"

"Oh, aye. How else will we season the meat?"

"Is there no brush?"

"No brush better than your hand." He demonstrated the process by sticking his thick fingers into the mixture and spreading it across the animal's tiny ribs. "Now you."

Shaking, I mimicked the action and rubbed some herbs onto the lamb's back. My nostrils flared wide as I cringed, but I was here to be useful. I'd make a lotion to undo the wrinkles later.

"Yes, like that. Good." He stepped away to finish chopping the cabbage.

I hesitantly pressed the herbs into the lamb with an unveiled expression of horror. The smell was disconcerting, and my stomach threatened to revolt as I touched raw flesh. Then, as I released my hand from the shoulder, the motion dropped the head forward, and a collection of bright red blood poured from the wound along the neck. In an instant, the lamb was not the lamb but my mother, her neck severed before me.

Snow had seen me go outside, against the king's rules, and into the sun. She had told the king. She had murdered my mother.

I had disobeyed the king, so Mother had been killed. Discarded. A tool that was no longer beautiful or useful.

My vision filled with blood and blackness. My throat constricted. As I fell, someone screamed. And the world went dark.

Chapter Fourteen

The Queen

Present day

Someone lifted my shoulder and laid me against a warm cloth. I stirred to prevent my head from snapping back as I was hoisted into the air. Something soft was placed behind me. The voices sounded muddled and far away but grew too loud as I blinked back the darkness.

"...herbs, who would have thought that it would result in this?"

"I'm not sure. Perhaps..." Damian's voice vibrated through his chest against my arm. He was holding me.

No.

With a sharp inhale, I sat straight up, nearly slamming my forehead into his face in my panic. My cheeks tingled, and my heart pounded in my chest; my vision darkened dangerously from sitting up too quickly.

"Whoa, easy," he said, reaching out to steady my shoulder.

I ignored the fuzzy edges to my sight as I held my head in my hands. "I'm fine."

His thumb drifted across my shoulder blade. "You collapsed, Lady Val."

"I did. But I'm alright now."

Damian met my gaze with his lips fully pressed and tilted. His look was filled with concern and thoughtfulness. "It seems the journey was too difficult for you. You should rest. I asked entirely too much of you on your first day. I'm sorry." He passed over a waterskin. "Please drink and rest."

"No, I'm fine, I'm sure I'm…" Hoisting myself up using the bench, I stood to prove I was okay. Half of the herbs had splattered onto the ground. I had worked so hard. "Oh, no." I rushed to pick up the bowl. "I'll fix this."

Chef stepped in to take it and set his stained hand on mine. "My lady, perhaps you should listen to—"

"It is you two who must listen to me," I said desperately, my mother's ghostly face still in my mind. "I am fine. I will remake the herbs. I…" I glanced over to the lamb for a second. "Or perhaps, you do the herb rubbing. It's too… I can't…" My eyes landed on the other table. "I can push on the bread dough instead…p-please?"

The two men shared a look before Chef nodded and passed me the bowl. "Alright. I'll gather the herbs."

Damian stood. His lips were still turned down, clearly displeased with me. "Lady—"

"I'm fine."

With a final huff, he turned and left with a flourish through the front flap.

Thankfully, the second time through the herb collection was finished quickly. The chef had already started the bread mixture and showed me how to knead the dough. The push and pull was somehow settling. I poked the bouncy substance with a mystified grin before I kneaded it again.

"Again, miss, push, don't punch the dough. You are a feisty thing, aren't you?"

A low chuckle seeped out of me. "Cooking is cathartic, it seems."

"That it is…if someone has a reason to need catharsis." His look was as piercing as Damian's. I clamped my lips shut, but he continued, "Even with me and the missus, at times, we all need to work through things. Dough is a good counselor."

"You are married?"

"Forty years. She is a seamstress in the castle, as lovely now as when we wed." His cheeks pinkened as he spoke, his voice as warm as the fire beside us. I paused in my work to study him. What would it be like to have someone be fond of me like he was of her? Neither my mother nor my husband had been. I had no child who had affection for me. An unbidden image of blue eyes, pale skin, and black hair with fat hands reaching for me flashed through my mind. Snow White, age four. Then her tackling hug, age nine, when she had fallen from the tree, and she buried her tearstained face in my chest. Perhaps she had loved me once.

I glanced up to find Chef staring at me as he added a log to the fire. I winced. "Did you say something?"

"Yes, but it doesn't matter. Your thoughts look heavy."

I bit my lip. "A bit."

"Heavy thoughts are lighter once shared." He came beside me to pinch the dough into spheres.

"Perhaps they are." I mimicked his actions. Thankfully, he let the moment rest.

"Well, you're a fast learner, and a master with the herbs," Chef said as he placed the dough into the frying pan. "You're welcome back anytime, even if it's not your night."

Pleasure bloomed in my chest, accompanied by a sense of accomplishment. Pride surged, but a quiet and new sense of gratitude bubbled past it. "Thank you, Chef. Thank you for teaching me." His wide grin radiated joy which overcame the imperfections of his haggard face and wayward teeth. It was...beautiful. I stared.

"Flip it in about four seconds," he said, drawing my attention down to the pan. "Three, two...ye—almost. Try it like this." He deftly tossed the bread, the bubbles of dough expanded and darkened. "Try again."

And I did.

As the men came to grab their meals, I rested with my back against the tent with Chef, enjoying how the fry bread pulled apart and how the honey dripped down its face, filling the crevasses and valleys. I wasn't sure I had ever enjoyed anything so good. Certainly, I'd had my fill of exotic desserts. But somehow, this was different. Earned. Peaceful. Shared. I exhaled slowly.

Caiden skipped to my side and sat in a puff of dust. He grinned at me as he tore into the food on his plate. "So, why'd you pass out."

I choked on a piece of bread.

"Caiden, manners," Damian hissed from the serving table.

Caiden ducked his head in apology. "Sorry, I mean, I heard you were unwell. How do you fare now, Lady Val?" My defense fizzled out at the expression on Caiden's face—he looked genuinely curious. It was hard to be angry at a puppy.

I brushed a crumb from my dress. "I'm well, thank you."

"Why did the lamb make you think of your mother?"

My eyes widened. "Excuse me?"

"We heard you yell for her. Perhaps you just wanted her. We all need our mothers when we are unwell. Is she at the castle? Are you close?" He bit into the lamb, a sluice of fat running down his chin. My appetite vanished.

"Still a bit nosy, brother." Damian said as he sat in front of us. "Although I wonder as well."

I glanced between the princes, wondering what I should say, but the best lies are couched in truth. "She was murdered, her neck slit in front of me. And the lamb...it was too similar." Both princes flinched, and somehow, I felt the pressure to continue on building within me. "It was the king. I...I disobeyed his order. She was...unkind. But she was still my mother."

"Was the king so brutal?" Damian asked, his voice low and growly.

I nodded. "And more so..."

Damian's expression was dark as he chewed his food, and even the boy prince was quiet. Damian continued, "I suppose I am grateful our trade agreements have been distant and straightforward, and that the union of our nations won't include such violence."

I studied the bread in my hands, picking it apart. Except that I may have accidentally killed the king...and deliberately poisoned the princess. "Yes. It is good you are here now."

Caiden raised his eyebrows and looked meaningfully at his brother, but when he received no response, he turned back to me. "Can you tell us a story about the princess? How about something from her childhood?"

I closed my eyes, trying to remember something worth telling. The silence stretched on, and Damian shifted his feet. I chose a memory at random. "Well, when the princess was seven, she hid a mother rabbit and her babies in her dollhouse for a full month." I smiled as I remembered. "She had cleaned all their messes by herself and stolen vegetables from the kitchen using the servant's passages. Her ruse was spoiled when she tried to put a baby bunny into her doll's gown, and it got stuck. She brought it to me to help her." I could still see her tear-stained cheeks as she shoved the pink-laced bunny in front of my face. "She insisted that we put them all in her doll house and move it into the gardens. The mother rabbit left immediately, so Snow kept caring for the babies, who also helped themselves to the garden. The chefs were furious, but then, what can you say to an adorable princess?"

Caiden's face split with a wide grin as he eyed his brother. "She sounds compassionate and sweet."

My heart gave a hard thump in my chest. Had she been? Memories flooded in, and I spoke them aloud: Snow scooping up the servant boy who had fallen off the garden wall. Snow tying her silk ribbon to a bent flower to heal it. Her misspelled notes and the thousands of pictures, the "drawlings," she had made for me.

Before the king placed her on a pedestal above everyone else. Before she told him I had disobeyed, and my mother had paid with her life. Before he used her to crush what little of me remained. Before she went along with him. Was it too much to ask her to resist him?

My heart thudded again.

But, had I?

CHAPTER FIFTEEN

The Mirror

Seven years earlier

I am the Mirror, and I would be shattered

To not witness hearts that are heaving and tattered.

To see evil deeds that mar beautiful souls,

Though I cannot see those, her acts display the holes.

The queen has not left her bed for three days. The king has commanded her to remain until she cleans the mess, but the queen has not stirred from her pillow. Though I am but the Mirror, I can see why.

Her mother's body still lies before me on the floor. Her vacant gaze stares at me along the wall. Accusing. Forgiving. Regretting. Saying nothing at all. Her face, once symmetrical, drifts to the floor; her cheek brackish purple on the stones. She curls around the brown puddle. The flies swirl above it all.

The queen lies as still as her mother. The sheets barely pull with each breath. The servants are not here and have not been since That Day.

Her face is before me as she holds her bedside mirror. The queen's face is not symmetrical now and marred by redness along her eyes and cheeks. Her lips are cracked.

She slowly lets out a breath. "Mirror, mirror, in my hand." The queen blinks, her gaze distant. "Who is the ugliest in the land?"

At once, I see through my thousands of reflections, onto thousands of faces.

"Mirror?"

"Though beauty is symmetry, ugliness is not a lack. And, my queen, there is other ugliness I now consider, though it is not all math and art. And there are many more of these. There is but one that is looking at me in the castle, right now. I have not considered him ugly, but I fear I must."

"The king?"

"He is nearly symmetrical, but..."

"But?"

"His ugliness is ever-present."

She whispers it back to me. "His ugliness is ever-present." A tear soaks into the pillow. "I would that I were ugly. Perhaps then..." Her voice catches. "Perhaps then, I would be free of him."

I say nothing about this because I cannot see. "Yet, you are not ugly," I say instead.

"Am I the fairest?"

"Is that the right question?"

"It has always been the only question."

The door slams and the king strides to the bed before the queen is able to tuck me under her pillow. He grasps her ankle, yanking her off the bed and onto the floor. He drags her toward her mother's still frame, near the dried blood that surrounds her.

"You will clean this. You will bathe. Then you will join me in my chambers."

The queen scrambles backward. "I cannot."

"You must."

She laughs darkly, low and hoarse. "You have nothing left to threaten me with."

The king pauses, then stoops to her face. "So help me Kevali, your life will be misery."

"It is already—"

He strikes her cheek, pointing a finger at her nose. "Though she is my blood, and she is lovely, she is still my tool, and I will hurt Snow White next if you do not do as you are told. I know you care for her."

The queen's jaw pops open, and she clasps her obsidian ring. "You wouldn't."

"Magic has made her, and magic can end her at my will. It is my right as King." He stands and stalks to the door, waving a hand flippantly. "I will sell her to Lord Baldwin."

The queen rises onto her elbow, her eyes wide. "He will beat her. He has killed his last five wives."

"All good husbands should keep their wives in line."

"She is eleven."

"That matters little to me or to Baldwin. Her fate is up to you, Kevali. Disobey me again, and I will destroy you both. Perhaps Baldwin can have you too. I will not need either of you anymore. You secured my throne and sealed the magic of the monarchy. My daughter would have continued my line, but after your mother had come so close, but failed to make me immortal, I am seeking other means. They will find a way. I will rule forever." His eyes flick around the room. "I'll send the captain for the body. He can dump it with the rest of the garbage. Then you finish it up." He points at her again, his eyes full of threats before he turns and leaves. The door slams and shakes me even through the stone.

The queen has no more tears. Moments pass before the door opens again. The captain looks at the scene for a moment with shock, then hardens his face as he wraps and removes the body of the queen's mother. The servants follow shortly with a lukewarm bath and a bucket of sudsy water.

"Start the fire." The queen says to one, who jolts at her words. She raises an eyebrow, and the servant complies.

The old blood is sticky, and the scrubbing is long. Fresh tears mingle with the red soap.

When her work is done, the queen strips bare and tosses everything into the fire. Her sheets and pillow burn as well. Her knees and hands are stained, and she looks from them to the fire, pausing too long. She cleans them with water from the cold bath instead.

The queen dips into the water wholly, her lips darken to a purple, and her skin erupts in goosebumps. But she does not hurry. Now, without blemish or stain, she stands before me naked. Her eyes observe every detail of her figure. She is more symmetrical now, and her skin tone is even, but her ribs are prominent, as are her cheekbones.

The queen's eyes are dry. She whispers, "Ever-present ugliness."

"My queen?"

"I will become like the king. Ever-present ugliness."

"But why? Who would choose to be ugly?"

"I am already ugly inside. Marred. Beyond salvaging. I am broken."

"You are symmetrical. You are fair."

"I am stained. I am poured out." She sighs. "But the princess—although she betrayed me, she is but a child." A tear brims at her lid, but she blinks it back with a sniff. "She will be more beautiful than me. And I hate her."

I see it all, and I don't believe her. "You are acting to save her."

"I will do whatever I must to survive, Mirror. And if it saves the princess, so be it. I will be fairest. I will be queen. I will win. He will lose. He did this."

She turns and slips into the low-cut wrap dress the king prefers. "I will harden. I will be as stone. More than before. It is too late for me. Even so, I will not let her go to Baldwin. I will not let her become as I am."

"But if you hate her, why would you protect the princess?"

Her gaze fixes on the flowering apple tree beyond the windowsill, her hand still on the tie of the belt. "Because, if there is beauty or hope or light that exists anywhere, perhaps there can be hope for me in the end.

"Once I'm free from him," she whispers. "Once I'm free."

CHAPTER SIXTEEN

The Queen

Present day

A fter two days of rear-numbing, back-aching, freckle-making riding, we finally arrived at the village by the forest. Caiden rode beside me and regaled me—for hours—with the inner workings of Zafmet's court, their trades, their local flora and fauna, their holidays, and their clothing preferences. Then, after hearing several more stories about Snow, he went through all the local noble gossip in detail. When Damian called for us to dismount, it would be a lie to say I was disappointed Caiden could not continue.

I bit my lip, focused on the steps Damian had showed me yesterday. Stand, stabilize, twist, and control the descent.

I did it.

Successfully dismounting from the horse, I spun with genuine delight. Right into Damian. Dousing the smile, I eyed his open arms, and found his face equally pleased. I would not stand to be mocked, but his wry eyebrow and kind smile held no malice or judgement. In fact, it looked sort of *proud*. A portion of my grin returned.

I was exemplary.

"Fast learner," he said as he began to untie my saddlebags. "That was exactly right. You even instinctually shifted your cloak and skirt from the horn and ties. I had forgotten to warn you about that yesterday." He pointed down to his worn riding trousers. "I have yet to ride a horse in a dress."

Fluffing my skirts caused a plume of dust to billow around my feet. "Well, you are missing out. Who does not want to bake under blankets and collect all these...plant pieces." Frowning, I picked off spikey puffs from the hem.

His laugh was genuine and full. "Perhaps I shall try it." He turned to me, his green-blue eyes glittering.

"Perhaps," I repeated with a smile of my own, as my heart flickered with...something.

"Perhaps what?" Caiden asked as he popped in front of my horse, tugging gently on the leads to tie her.

Damian looked pointedly at me in warning, and I stifled my grin. He turned to Caiden. "Perhaps nothing. My lady, you are free tonight. My squadron is set to trace the perimeter and scout for first shift. Caiden is on kitchen duty. And the others are setting up camp and caring for the horses."

I tapped my foot, unwilling to be on my own. "Can...can I help cook?" But just as I uttered the words, three newly slaughtered goats and rabbits were carried past us toward the beginnings of a fire. Damian gently turned my shoulder toward the tents. I allowed the guidance.

"Not tonight, Lady Val. Caiden has it covered."

Looking at the large group of men setting up tents, I rolled my shoulders. "Alright, I'm coming with you then."

Damian froze. "My lady, scouting is one of the most dangerous—"

I waved off the rest of his sentence. "I will not remain here alone."

"It is not safe."

I turned to him with a high eyebrow. "Are you saying that you will not keep me safe?"

Dark eyebrows matched his dark expression. "Of course I would, but—"

"Then it's decided.'"

Caiden watched us with wide eyes, unbridled amusement, and cautious concern as he waited for his brother's response. Damian crossed his arms. "Your dresses will be noisy, in the way, and—and will collect more seeds."

"I will..." Clearing my throat, I tried again. "I will wear trousers."

He snorted in an unprincely way. "Did you bring any trousers? Do ladies here own trousers?"

I glanced around rapidly, my hand waving between us as I tried to come up with a solution to the problem I'd just created. "I...well...perhaps... I'm certain there may be a spare pair around here."

Damian's cocky grin returned. "And which of my men would lend a lady of the court trousers?"

From behind my horse, a pair of leather trousers flew and slapped loudly upon Damian's shoulder. The young prince's head popped above the saddle. "I have some!"

"Caiden!" The elder prince glared daggers at the younger.

"Oops, got to go find Chef. Time to cook. So long, my lady!" Caiden said with a broad grin as he scampered away.

Before Damian could snatch them, I plucked the trousers off his shoulder. "These will work."

The steps of the approaching soldier pulled my attention to him. My erected tent stood just behind and surrounded by a circle of the elite soldiers' tents as it has since the start of our journey, and yet, it had become no less terrifying...or isolating. I couldn't stay here. Glancing back to Damian, I smiled. "I'll be right back."

"I'm not waiting for you. We need to go now," Damian called after me.

"Then I will wander until I find you." I had my back to him but still felt his anger rising like the sun on my back. His steps crunched through the dry grass behind me. He pulled on my shoulder, softer than I had braced for so I turned back. Though his face was serious, I felt no mortal danger.

"As the eldest prince and leader of this party, I command you to stay. My lady, I will not put your life at risk. There could be wolves, or bears, or...ruffians..."

His protective words, so much like Yates's, caused something to warm in my chest. But I was done crumpling or cowering to commands. Fake lady's maid or not, I had suffered under obstinate men and would stand against any other. I sighed from the fatigue of fighting it all. I was tired from the journey, tired of pretending everything was okay, and most of all, tired of being alone.

My voice quieted, weary but sure as I met his gaze. "My decision is yes. I don't want to stay here."

An unprincely sound erupted from his throat as he wheeled toward the fire. Several soldiers skipped aside as he stormed past. As I pulled open my tent, I glanced back to see Damian pointing toward me while he spoke to Caiden. I twiddled my fingertips at them, amused at the deepening furrow of Damian's eyebrows. Who knew they could go any lower?

I stepped inside and began to change before I realized a few things at once: I had no shirt, only long shifts and lengths of skirts and gowns. Furthermore, Caiden was not made with wide hips and these trousers would not rise over my curves. Despite my twisting and turning, the trousers would not go on. Worst of all, I was starting to wonder if Damian was right and I should stay at the camp instead of rushing off in foolishness. I held the trousers briefly before I threw them to the ground. It looked like I would have to stay here.

I winced as I realized I needed to relieve myself.

I looked out the tent and stared at the forest. Wolves, and bears, and ruffians. A shiver followed the ice that trickled down my back. I was so tired of being afraid. I grabbed my small shoulder bag and slipped away from the tents. Only one soldier stopped and approved my forest venture. Damian had already left to scout.

A hundred paces into the woods, I could no longer see the sides of the tents and found a place to hide myself. The forest was very quiet, eerily so, and I wondered if I should have brought the embarrassed soldier. I didn't want to be alone, and Damian was long gone. A queen, disguised as a lady-in-waiting, fit as well in the quiet forest as leather shoes in lemon cream pie.

Stepping away from my hiding spot, I took in the solitude of the moment. Everything that caused me to end up here. I shook my head and turned back to the camp which was fully obscured by the trees. Patting the bag that held my potion vials, I was reminded that even if I got lost, I would still have enough for a few days. The rest remained tucked in my clothes at the tent. Safe and sound.

A stick snapped to my right, and I ducked behind a flimsy bush.

One minute passed, then another. Silence. I let out a slow breath. A massive hand clamped over my mouth and my body exploded in panic. Throwing an elbow backward, I bit down hard and wrenched away. Landing on my rear, I skittered backward. As my eyes landed on the attacker, my heart stuttered.

Oops.

"Curses, woman!" Damian whispered as he shook his wounded hand. "I mean, my lady. Get back here. Quietly!"

My face burned with shame as I willed my heartbeat to slow. I slunk back toward Damian, and he pressed me to the side, with a nod toward the bushes.

"Hide. Something is coming."

Tucking myself into the shadows, he followed, keeping himself between me and the outside. When nothing happened, and his attention stayed focused ahead of us, I relaxed a fraction. This man was not *that man.*

Beside me, tiny pat-pat-pats, hit the dry pine needles below. I sucked a breath through my teeth and snatched his hand.

"You're bleeding," I whispered, horrified.

Damian glanced down and shrugged. "So it seems."

I extracted a handkerchief from my bag and dabbed at the crescent wound. One seeping mark for each tooth. The bite mark arced on each side of the pulp of his palm.

"I-I'm s—" The word caught in my throat. "You snuck up on me. I..." I clamped my lips shut and focused on wrapping his injury.

Moments passed, but only wildlife disturbed the quiet sounds of sunset. Damian stood and offered his other hand to help me rise. Why wasn't he angry with me?

Tilting his head toward a deer path, he gently pulled me behind him as he continued scouting. "My lady, you are too reckless. I only wanted to keep you safe."

I slipped my hand out of his grip. "I only came out here to relieve myself, Damian. Besides, I have spent decades being kept *safe*." I spat out the last word, so vile and toxic on my tongue.

As his brows furrowed, I realized I had kept walking when he had stopped, and now I stood within inches of his shoulder. He turned, and we stood chest to chest, my face tilted up toward his. I ignored the heat on my cheeks as I tried to move past him. He reached for my arm, and I hesitated with a twitch.

His light eyes were too piercing as they searched mine, his face all empathetic concern. "I'm not going to hurt you."

I snorted. "I'm not scared of you."

His lips pulled to the side in disbelief before he stepped back an inch. He looked me over as he spoke in a low, rough voice. "If you flinch every time I reach to touch you, then you were never safe." He set his hand on my shoulder, and I couldn't suppress the shudder that rippled through my muscles. His frown deepened. "Not safe at all."

Sudden, stinging, angry tears burned at the corners of my lids, and I ducked under his hand. At once, I felt very vulnerable and very *seen*. I was ready to start moving. Stepping into a large clearing, I said, "You'd better get back to your"—my hands waved in the air—"patrol. Scouting. Whatever."

A twang preceded a woody thunk as a red-feathered arrow struck the tree several steps before me. The prince ripped out his sword and faced the origin of the weapon. Beside us on the other side, a voice, just as sharp and deadly, called out, "I would put that sword down now, if I were you."

Emerging like wraiths behind us, three men slipped from the shadows of the trees, dressed in muddy green and black leather. The man who called out emerged with two others. All six had arrows pointed right at us.

Damian started to set down his sword, one hand up in surrender.

The man gestured between us. "And no signaling for help. Or you'll get it."

I glared with equal parts embarrassment and anger. We were surrounded, and it was my fault. "The only thing I will get is my dinner."

Damian's eyes widened while the shadowed speaker's eyes crinkled on the sides. "The lady is mouthy."

The chuckle that rumbled through the group of men sent warning shivers down my spine. I stiffened my shoulders. "The lady is hungry. And if you'll excuse us, we are headed to get some food."

"The lady has trespassed on our land."

"This land belongs to the queen and to the sovereign nation of Acacia." I tilted my chin.

The man lowered his bow and gestured around the forest. "I don't see a queen here, do you?" My lips tightened. He continued. "We follow a policy of finders keepers. We found you, and therefore, we keep you." The moonlight glittered on his exposed teeth. His gaze flicked toward Damian. "Toss down that dagger as well. And the one in your boot."

Damian complied with a growl. "My men will find you and track you down. This will not end well for you."

"Says the one who did not sense us in the first place."

Damian's jaw twitched, his chest heaving in suppressed tension. The bowmen shifted their bows toward him. For some reason, I stepped in front of him.

"You seem like...reasonable, if not overly armed humans. Can we negotiate?"

White teeth glinted from within the shadows as the man smiled. "Sure. We take you to our camp. You stay quiet. Deal."

CHAPTER SEVENTEEN

The Mirror

Five years earlier

I am the mirror, and knowledge is sharp.

The cost is too high, when no change I can impart.

To see all and know all, I wish I were blind.

Or sleeping, or hiding, some of the time.

The queen has not paused her pacing since the debutante ball except to pour through her spell book. She whips through the pages, back and forth, muttering out loud, but not to me.

"He would kill me if he found out."

"Just a little spell..."

"But the magic, would it protect him?"

"Did mother's death release the shield?"

But I remain silent.

Across the castle I see Snow White sitting before me in her room, brushing her hair. She idly picks up a pearl barrette. A tear drips down her cheek. Her beauty remains but is marred by the line between her brows. She is here daily when no one else is around. Her words are the same.

"She could never forgive me."

"How could I be so foolish?"

"I miss her..."

In another room, the king plans his evening with his butler. His hands upon his cravat tie even as they shake from lack of drink.

"Be sure they all come, Yates, my men need entertainment."

"Kevali's face? Ha! Worthless, spineless..."

"I never drink to excess, Yates, mind your tongue."

The queen sets her hands against the columns on each side of my face and asks again. "Mirror, mirror, on the wall, who is the fairest of them all?"

"My queen, I say once more, the princess is more lovely, as when you asked before."

"Mirror, mirror, on the wall, when my mother died, did her magic fall?"

I pause, since the magic lays thick throughout the castle, and it is hard to see. "The charms you wrote and painted there, remain intact, without impair...ment. The magic is fading, that much I can see, but a test of their strength might be just what you need."

Her eyes are wild, their whites exposed as her teeth glisten in a smile that is not lovely. "Then a test I shall make."

The queen returns to her spell book and black cauldron, and begins pulling potions and leaves from the shelves. "The way is clear to me now. Perhaps a bit of embarrassment would be good for the king. If he wishes to magic his way to a beautiful daughter, and use his power to flaunt his women, then he can also have a dose of his own public shame...

"Just a bit of vomit, I think. Perhaps the other end as well for good measure." She laughs, but it is not musical. Then sneaking through the servant passage, past the kitchen and into the king's trophy room, the queen slips the potion into the king's chalice.

I watch her from above the fireplace, this new ugliness.

"If the potion works, Mirror, then we will know. Then we can see if I can harm his and his blood. Just a little. Just a bit of justice. Though he will be made a fool, they will think him only drunk, and no one will be the wiser."

Then with what I could only call a cackle, the queen slips back into the shadows of the corridor.

Chapter Eighteen

The Queen

Present day

W alking to the rebel camp seemed nigh impossible. My thighs, already raw from riding, scraped together as my feet throbbed and seared like I had been stepping on coals. I was only stopped from falling on my face by the soldier who wrenched my bound arms behind me every time I stumbled. The farther we traveled, the more frequently I tripped. I held my head as high as ever, but my body failed to follow the commands. How infantile that my thighs could not lift my boots above the brush? Would I crawl next? I wondered if I should release the disguise and release my bound magic with it, exposure to Damian be damned. But we had to wake the princess. I would wait to unfurl my magic for now.

The leader moved like a cat on the prowl. He had pulled back his hood, and in the moonlight, my eyes drifted down every fold of twisted scar tissue on his cheek and neck, curled like the portraits of the volcano flows that dotted our continent's southern shoreline. Each crevasse was filled with dirt and ash. His neck pulled taut as he turned to me, unnaturally folding like untreated leather. Stiff and rigid.

Tripping again, I fell to the ground and cried out as the soldier lifted me up by my hands.

"Stop it. You'll dislocate her shoulders," Damian spat. "She's a lady."

The soldier dropped my hands, and therefore me, back on the ground. I hit with a thud, knocking the wind from my lungs. "She is not *my* lady," the man grumbled.

"Mason. Pick the woman up. We are not the monsters here," the leader said. The man glared at the leader but reached for me.

Fear clenched my gut, and I writhed away, gathering the remaining dregs of energy to shove myself back onto my knees. "Do not touch me."

Mason gaped at the leader with raised brows and two open palms gesturing at me. The leader tilted his head toward me again.

"I said, do not touch me!" I rose on my own with a grunt, glaring at Mason. "Do not touch me ever again."

A sigh before me drew my attention. The leader stood but a few feet ahead, his hands on his hips. He flicked a glance to our guard. "To the front. I'll walk them."

Mason saluted sloppily with a "Yes, Captain," before loping to the front like a werewolf, bent and gangly. I turned my sneer to my captor.

"You don't get to touch me either."

He observed me for a moment before he began to walk, triggering the whole company to shift forward down the path. "Is it more desirable for you to end up with a face full of dirt?"

My laugh was bitter. "Infinitely. If I am never touched by a man again, it will be too soon."

The leader shrugged off my comment. "Why are you in the forest?"

"Why should we tell you?"

"Because your traveling party is marked with the queen's insignia, and you have been captured and bound and are walking to your imprisonment?"

I snorted ruefully. "There are worse things than that too."

This time his brow furrowed.

"Besides," I continued, "I don't know what side you are on, what your goals are, or if you have a mission apart from kidnapping, pillaging, plundering, and other criminal behaviors."

"We weren't always criminals, you know. Some of us even worked at the castle. Under the king...then under the queen."

My step faltered. I didn't recognize them.

"But things went badly, then even worse. So we set off on our own and met a kind benefactor. You'll meet him tomorrow. Maybe I should thank the queen for all this. Without her, I would have never found this crew, never found the greater purpose of serving our people. At the castle, I was surviving, but out here"—he threw his arms wide open—"I am thriving and free. Our mission is to save our country before the queen lets it burn to the ground." He snorted. "Or lets the floods wash it away. Or ignores our allies."

Thoughts whirled through my mind, a thousand defenses surging to my lips. But what defense was there when much of what he said was true? Exhausted, my shoulders collapsed.

Quietly, I said, "It's not the queen's fault there is a drought in the north that led to the fires. It's not her fault the floods from a wayward monsoon from the coast took out the bridge to Helene and her supplies from our neighbors. It's not the queen's fault that the soldiers who could have been deployed to save the villages were destroyed in the king's last attempt to conquer L'Hovat and their raiders at the border. Nor is it her fault that the country's agriculture infrastructure is poised but on the edge of a knife or that her treaties are not fulfilled by her allies to the west." Quieter still, I whispered. "And it is not her fault that she was poisoned by degrees by the toxic king."

The forest was silent. The wind itself held its breath. I paused to see the soldiers, our captor, and Damian all staring at me with wide, bewildered expressions.

The leader stepped toward me. "And how does a lady's maid come to know of such things?"

I met his gaze with my own intensity. "It is easy to be forgotten when you are a background design feature. A living portrait. A walking, commissioned statue. People are always underestimating the silent and observant."

Mason muttered from the front. "This lady has hardly been silent."

I glared at him as the men fell into quiet laughter. Heat burned my cheeks.

The leader smiled, and his smile didn't hold the mockery of the others. "As a guard to the king, I understand the sentiment. I am glad you did not hold back your opinions, as misguided and protective of the queen as they are. It is clear you love our people."

I loved my people? My lips tipped down. "I know my duty."

"Well, perhaps we are not as opposed in our missions as I had believed." He scratched his beard, plucking out a piece of leaf as we all headed into a wide meadow. Tents and portable structures lined the edges.

"Ah, we've arrived at your lodgings," the man said as he approached a large, thick pole in the center of the circle. He sat us down, then fastened me and Damian to the pole with a series of knots that were too fast to follow. My hands, still bound, ached as they were squeezed against the roughened wood.

Panic bloomed in my stomach. I hated being bound. "I-I would like some water."

"I would like the queen to face justice. We all want things that we don't have."

"Perhaps, then, you can have mercy and give me my medicine. It's in the pouch on my side."

The man paused. "Medicine? For what?"

"My history is my own. Just one vial."

"I think not."

"I have a...a weak constitution and...and nerves, sir. I need my medicine." Panic crawled up my spine. I calculated the time that remained before I turned back into myself. "I *need* it." The man's lips tilted unhappily, but he reached to open my pouch. From the sound of clattering glass, I knew what he had found. My heart dropped into my gut.

"It seems your medicine vials are broken, my lady." With a patronizing pat on my head, he turned to his tent. "There is nothing better for nerves than nature, and there is nothing weak about you." With a backward wave, he pulled open his tent door. "Sleep tight, now!" He disappeared inside with a crack of canvas.

I kicked a rock awkwardly on the ground in front of me, angry and scared. I was going to be found out. I would transform right here in the middle of this encampment tomorrow or the next day, tied to this cursed pole. Blonde one minute, redheaded the next. Innocent now, guilty later. I would be executed by those who hated me. My terror made me furious. "Of all the insolent, disrespectful..."

Damian's chuckle rumbled from behind me. "Were you expecting a bunch of law-abiding, considerate, and generous ruffians in the woods?"

My lip protruded just a bit. "No, but...but my medicine..."

Damian hummed. "In that one aspect, he was correct. You are not weak."

I bit my lip, the memories pouring in from my life—a thousand acts of blatant cowering filtered through my mind. An entire *lifetime* of weakness and subjugation. Though it was my desire to never be weak again, the truth was barely veiled, exposed by the memories and realities of my existence. I knew who I was and who I had been. I knew the depths of my incompetence and mistakes. I knew that I was weak. Unbidden tears lined my lids. I sniffed them back.

"May I?" Warmth suddenly wrapped around my fingertips as Damian shifted sideways to grasp what he could of my hands. A huff of air escaped me; I was surprised by how much comfort I felt from his touch. Heat prickled up my back and burrowed into my chest and cheeks. I lay my head back against the wooden stake as I slowly inhaled. I would riddle through this sensation later.

He fiddled gently with my black gem ring. "We will make it out of this, my lady. I will do whatever I must to keep you safe. My men will come for us shortly."

For some idiotic reason, I believed him. I shifted a finger against the rough calluses of his palm. "And the princess?"

"Well," he squeezed my hands again. "I hope we can rescue her, too, and find our party. But first, we need to save ourselves."

As he pulled away, a wisp of cold wind laced through my fingers.

"Wait." I grimaced at how desperate I sounded. "Don't let go just yet. Please."

The heat returned, and his thumb gently caressed a fingertip. The panic that had gripped my heart eased slightly. His voice rumbled. "As the lady wishes."

CHAPTER NINETEEN

The Mirror

Five years earlier

I am the mirror, and in life there are lines,

Moments and decisions that turn arms of time.

Small steps, at first, soon become a great leap.

The cost of those choices becomes much too steep.

The king is sick.

The queen's glee would have almost looked lovely, if it did not also curve her cheek sharply at her nose, raised in contempt. She rested in her chaise, in the shadows at the edge of the light from her window. Her fingers drift across her mother's pearls, counting the beads and recounting the lives they'd once held.

The queen has never made pearls of her own.

A knock at the door does not stir her.

"My queen?" The butler enters and clasps his vest within his blanching fingers.

"What news of the king?"

He clears his throat once. And again. "The king worsens. Another physician and yet another magician have been called. The leeches were removed this morning, Your Majesty."

"Ah. Leeches...what a pity for the king. The woman from the Isle left?"

"This morning, my queen. Her carriage left at first light."

The queen turns her head to meet his gaze, and her eyes glimmer with pleasure. "Excellent." She waves a hand toward her desk. "I have made the king a potion for the nausea. It should help, I think."

Yates nods and grasps the glass container. The boiling blue liquid bubbles within. Bowing, he turns and rushes to the king.

The queen returns to her outdoor vigilance.

"My queen," I ask, "you act to help the king?"

She flips her full red hair over her shoulder. "Only a bit. The goal, my mirror, was to prove that my magic could finally affect him, to shame him, and to rid my castle of others who would take my place as queen." An ugly scoff clears her throat. "Bedfellows are certainly shameful, but it keeps me out of his room, so I shall permit his private dalliances. But I will not tolerate a usurper. My mother fought hard for magic to have its place in this kingdom, and to set me on the throne. I will not lose it now." The queen laughs. "Even with all his misguided attempts at immortality..."

Yates offers the potion to the king, who paws at it with greed in his sallow, yellowed eyes. Choking down the liquid, the king sighs with relief. But it does nothing to stop the wet and putrid cough.

A knock sounds on the queen's door before she has stirred from her bed the next morning. Yates enters the room. "My queen."

Stretching, the queen rolls toward him. "What news of the king? Did he take my potion?"

Yates nods, before he takes his handkerchief to his forehead. "The king has not vomited since your kind gesture. But my queen, he calls for you. The physicians...Majesty, they think it is the end."

The queen sits up. "The end? But it was only a stomach sickness!"

"The king coughs, his temperature climbs, he sees wraiths in the room, and he hears music that doesn't exist."

"Coughs," the queen repeats. "Coughs? Why was I not called before this?"

The butler pulls at his collar. "The king did not want your help then..."

"But now he calls for me."

I watch the other room and speak the truth. "He calls for your hair, my queen."

Yates turns to me, red tinging his wrinkled cheeks, before shifting back toward the queen. "It is as the mirror says, my queen."

"Of course," she says, a hiss lingering at the end.

The queen enters the room with a shaking hand. Her nose crinkles at the smell of the room as she takes in the potions, the nurses, and the magicians that line the room. They speak in groups, whispering harshly about finding new cures, new things to try on the sickly monarch. But I hear every word: they have nothing more to try.

The queen steps beside the bed and sits in the chair brought for her.

"Kevali," he whispers.

"My king." Her eyes fall on the bedside table, and she withdraws suddenly upon seeing the dagger, the runes, and the corpse of the chicken. She gasps. "Blood magic?"

He wheezes a laugh, and green spittle lands on his lips, dripping with the rest of his sweat down his chin. "Even blood magic won't save me, it seems. Unbind your hair."

The queen does as he commands, and he pulls it weakly toward him. He rubs the ruby strands between his fingers. "This was always your best feature."

The furrow between her brows almost softens.

"But it will never be as lovely as hers is now."

He pulls her hair tighter and tighter, drawing her closer until her face is before him. She turns her face away. "You will have nothing when I go. I have signed the papers. I have sealed the contracts. Yates will be regent upon my death, and Snow will be queen on her 18th birthday. And you will rest upon her mercy. You may keep your room, but you will perform no duties. You will be as you have always been...worthless, useless, pointless. Your magic tools will be confiscated, and your windows sealed shut. In the place where your mother bled out, you will remain. You will be caged until Death pulls you with me." He attempts a laugh. "If only I could have Death take you with me now."

The queen lurches back, her head yanked to the side as she overcomes his weak grip.

The king continues, "But it is better this way. From the beyond I will watch you suffer. And I will rest in peace." His laugh turns to racking coughs, and the nurses rush beside him to dab his forehead and prop up his pillow. Then his eyes glaze over, a pool of drool leaks from his lips, and as he stares vacantly at the queen, the light in his eyes flickers unto death.

Hours later, the queen sits before me. Silent. Unblinking.

"I must...he can't...could he?" She questions the room but not me.

"Mirror."

"My queen."

"I have nothing." She inhales slowly. "I am nothing."

I begin to speak but she continues, "His reach stretches beyond the grave. Putting her, that child, that murderess—in word if not in deed, but murderess none the less—upon my throne." Her eyes flutter closed. "Removing my magic. Locking me in. Taking my hope of freedom..."

I try to interject the truth of the princess's regret and guilt. "But the princess—"

"The princess hasn't spoken to me since That Day. She hates me as she did."

"This is not true." I try again.

"What is truth where there is only darkness."

Regarding herself in the mirror, she tilts her chin down, and her eyes narrow to slits. "Ever-present ugliness."

"My queen?"

"Mirror, I must destroy the signed papers." Her fingers clench upon a pearl barrette. "And then I must kill the princess. I have essentially killed the king. But his death will not release me. Only when I'm alone will I be free...

"When I'm alone, then I will be free."

Chapter Twenty

The Queen

Present day

I hadn't expected to sleep while sitting bound and strained but found myself waking to the sound of the dawn birds. My toes were cold, but my hands were warm. "Oh, it's morning," I whispered. We had made it. Alive. I tossed my head; I was still blonde.

Damian's rough voice brushed past me like a caress. "Aye, that it is. I often find that morning comes after the night."

I snorted in an unladylike way, the edges of my lips attempting a smile. "Have you really? You are extraordinarily observant."

"I am known to be a genius in my lands." His morning voice was growly, and somehow, I found it soothing. It stirred a sensation I didn't recognize.

"A well-earned title, I am sure." I shifted, trying to relieve my sore rear and numb foot. My hands were still coiled within his. My heart hammered in a moment of indecision before pressing into the warmth of his palms. They were massive, strong, rough, and no doubt had dealt out their share of violence. But had anyone ever held me with such gentleness? Perhaps not all strength was dangerous.

He broke through my thoughts with a long exhale. "So what's a lady like you doing in a rebel camp like this?"

The laugh that escaped was surprising and entirely too loud. I fought to stifle it before I woke someone up. "I bet you say that to all the ladies you are tied up with."

His chuckle was the most beautiful sound I had ever heard. "Well, it may surprise you to hear this, but this is my first time."

"Hmm."

"It's not as bad as I expected."

I frowned and counted all the spots that ached, burned, and prickled from our positioning. "Is that so?"

"Quite. I'd expected to be beaten by now. Instead, I got to rest my feet, hold your hands, and tell you bad jokes. All in all, a very pleasant kidnapping."

"The day is still young. You could still experience a myriad of new things." I shuddered slightly at the thought, and he squeezed my fingers softly.

"Ach, I doubt it. But even still, as long as they don't hurt you, I'll be alright."

My throat tightened at a sudden wave of emotion. The king had been obsessive, jealous, and reactive against outsiders. He was protective like a dragon over his hoard. He didn't act like this man—treating me like I was a real person, someone worth protecting. My voice cracked. "Well, if it's all the same to you, I'd rather they don't hurt you either."

"I'll do my best to charm them with my sweeping good looks and plethora of great jokes."

I smiled. "You're sure to woo them with those."

"So you think me charming and good looking too?"

I squawked, caught off guard. "I...I... Well..."

Crunching rocks interrupted my flailing. Glancing up into the early eastern light, our captor approached and stopped, standing with his feet apart. Light reflected off a massive ax, which he pulled back and, with a grunt, accelerated toward me. My eyes widened, but no words escaped.

My end would be as ignoble as the rest of my life. The ax—like the hand, the belt, the fist, and the insult—would land on me, hurting me, weakening me. Like every time before, I froze; I flattened my face and stared my attacker down with a stony expression. My fingers twitched for my ring, but they were still held tightly in the warm grasp behind me.

Yet, when the ax struck, I felt no pain. Only a release in my lungs. Did he strike my chest? I inhaled more freely. My hands tingled in my demise.

"Are you going to get up, or are you going to stare at me like a porcelain doll all day?" the leader scoffed.

I blinked once. "What?"

He set the ax-head down and leaned on the wooden handle like a cane. "I cannot undo your wrists if you do not move. So what will it be, dear lady?"

Glancing down, I saw the ropes had been cut and coiled onto my lap. Damian shuffled beside me and looked me over with concern. Finding no blood or injury, he turned his shoulder to let the man undo his binds.

"Next." He flipped a knife in his hand casually, as Damian rubbed his wrists. I barely shifted, but it was enough to let him slice through the ropes.

Damian stood and offered me his hand, which I accepted to pull myself up to my feet. But when I was upright and stable, I found I didn't want to let go. I gripped his fingers and turned to the man. "Why are you releasing us?"

"I'm untying you, not releasing you. It's time for breakfast. That benefactor I mentioned, Johannes, he wants to speak with you." He led us before a makeshift table as a massive man with dark hair and chocolate skin emerged from an ornately decorated tent. Archers stood around him, twenty men lining the circle.

"Sir, these are the two I told you about."

The man looked me over, raising a brow as he regarded our clasped hands before flicking his gaze over to Damian. His brows collapsed in confusion. "Prince Damian?"

"Johannes... *Prince* Johannes?" Damian said. My eyes widened as I desperately tried to place his name among the neighboring countries. Who was invading my lands now?

The man approached rapidly, greeting Damian with a handshake and slapping hug. "It has been years, *years*! Where is that ankle biter, baby Caiden?" Johannes glanced at me. "And who is this?"

Damian turned and took my hand in the royal fashion. "May I present Lady Val." Damian looked as if he would say more but glanced about the group of armed rebels. "Why are you here? Did they capture you too?"

Johannes snorted. "I hired them. They are good men. Stinky. But good. Come. Let's eat. My friend here conveyed the lady's words from yesterday. I believe we have some matters we should discuss. Sorry about the whole"—he waved his hands—"kidnapping and night tied to a pole. If I had known..." He glared at the leader who turned red before hustling off.

I turned sharply to Damian. "Did you plan this whole thing?"

Prince Johannes cackled. "Now that would be some planning! Lady, he is clever, but no one could have predicted this. The stars have aligned and ordained our reunion!" He pointed to a table. "Come, come. Let us eat together."

Damian smiled at him before turning to me. "I promise on my throne that I had no idea Prince Johannes was here and did not plan this."

I searched his face, wishing I could ask the mirror, but for some reason, I believed him. At least, a little.

CHAPTER TWENTY-ONE

The Queen

Present day

Round logs served as seats around the makeshift table as some of the men brought over potato hash with pork belly, lemon dressed greens, and soft fried eggs. The seasonings were foreign but amazing. My heart ached as I thought of my starving people.

Johannes noticed my appreciative gaze. "If you think the food is good, try this." A bright silver kettle poured steaming black liquid into tiny silver cups.

As he moved to another cup, Damian leaned forward with a deep sniff. "Of course! I remember this, but it was so long ago."

"Kafke," Johannes supplied, "the elixir of youth and vitality. From the finest beans of L'Hovat. Drink and let us have peace."

The dawning revelation was slow, but icy. Johannes was L'Hovian. Of course. The enemy in the east that our general was fighting. A hundred stories of L'Hovian hostility came to mind: how they refused to trade, stole our land, and killed my armies. I glanced toward Damian again, wondering if he was going to double-cross me and betray me to our enemies.

Johannes continued as he poured, "If you have the ear of the queen, as the Captain seems to believe, and since you"—he filled Damian's cup—"are the prince of Zafmet, and I am the youngest son of the king of L'Hovat, then we now have ourselves a right political peace convention."

I reached for the offered cup, wondering for a brief moment if it was poison before Johannes took a sip of his own. I sipped the bitter liquid. "I didn't think the princes ever left the capital, let alone their country." Johannes glanced at me, then down at my round black ring, halting for a moment before he set the kettle down.

"Well, my obsidian lady, we most often do not. Until a country forces mine to investigate or conquer." His words were hard, and his gaze harder. But after a moment, both softened to display curiosity. "And why does an educated lady ride with a prince of a foreign nation on the opposite side of the land from the capital? You are both too close to this conflict and without an army to protect you." His expression to Damian was also disapproving.

I shot a hesitant glance at Damian, who nodded his encouragement. "The prince is going to save the princess. I was accompanying them to her location."

Johannes's dark eyebrows disappeared into his tightly twisted hair. "Oh? The dead princess? And how will he do that? Through necromancy?" Laughter rippled through the men on the periphery.

I swallowed. "She yet lives, though she sleeps. The prince will kiss her, and she will awaken. Once they marry, we shall form a treaty with Zafmet." I cleared my throat. "The queen will form a treaty with his father, that is. And they shall trade and help our people."

"If we hold him for ransom, those funds would help the people more," he said smoothly, with a wink at Damian.

I turned to him, irritation heating my blood. "Ransom funds cannot stop the flooding or the fires, nor will they feed our people long term. They cannot eat metal if we have no allies to sell us what we need. We have all the mining resources that they could possibly want. But gems are not food. If you do not let us go, you will create more enemies for Acacia.

Then you will be responsible for the further starvation of our people. Your solution is short-sighted and may trigger a war our countries cannot afford." When I was finished, I realized I had been goaded. Johannes smiled at me, and Damian searched my face thoughtfully.

"Just so," Johannes said, his fingers scratching his chin. "In this vein, my obsidian lady—"

"Lady Val."

"Perhaps, but you are all obsidian." His eyes glanced back down to my ring. I frowned in confusion, but before I could clarify, he spoke. "The nation of L'Hovat wonders why the nation of Acacia refuses to treat. Certainly, a treaty would relieve the strain your war is causing upon the people and your resources."

"Acacia has never refused to treat—that is, under the queen. It is L'Hovat that has refused every overture and extension of peace."

Johannes extended a stiff and flattened hand, slicing through the air in the first sign of frustration. "This is absolutely untrue. For years, my father has reached out, even as your soldiers invaded our lands."

"Invaded? Your soldiers keep taking our borders and killing off our patrols."

Johannes bristled, but Damian raised two fingers to speak. "Perhaps, my lady, you are not as well informed as you thought."

My spine stiffened in offense. I had sat through multiple meetings under the king. I had been informed of these offenses by the general over the last few years. But Damian's expression stilled me. I took a breath and asked, "How do you mean?"

Damian leaned forward, elbows on the table. "I mean that what Johannes says is the truth. For years, Acacia has broken the Century Peace Plan and stolen L'Hovat's land. We sent an envoy to their border just before we arrived at the castle to confirm it. To see who we were negotiating trade with for ourselves." He rubbed his chin. "The violations were almost enough to nullify this whole agreement."

Johannes sipped his kafke again. "It is only because of our commitment to peace and our hope of discussions with the queen that all-out war has not been brought to your front door. But my father is growing impatient that his messages are not returned."

"There have been no messages..." I started, flicking my eyes between the men. All somber. All watching me. "The general..." I squeezed my hands, wringing them together in my lap as I remembered every inflammatory accusation he had leveled against L'Hovat. Every request for increased violence. Every manipulation of me and my throne and my army. While I had suspected the general disagreed with my ideas, I hadn't realized he would lie to accomplish his own violent goals.

Fury boiled within me as I took a steadying breath, then released it like steam from the kafke kettle. "I am certain that the queen did not know and has been misinformed regarding the state of the border. I know that the queen desires peace and stability throughout her land." I turned more fully toward Johannes. "I am also certain the queen will treat with you. However, I am not certain her military leaders would allow you to pass in peace. Not until she deals with them."

"Which is why I ride with rebels and rejects. Your general has been particularly hard to contact and violent to our messengers."

Damian reached for more kafke. "Perhaps Zafmet could serve as a neutral center for peace discussions."

"Have to get us through Gotsburg," Johannes said.

I swirled the liquid in my tiny silver cup. "We are on good terms with Gotsburg, though. They have more love for our gems than anything else."

Johannes raised his glass. "Then to peace."

The others lifted their glasses to the center. I fiddled with my own. "To—well, in as much as this lady can offer her promises—to peace. Acacia, L'Hovat, and Zafmet." I pushed mine forward too.

The men's gazes met for a moment. Then we drank.

Damian studied the dark liquid he swirled in his cup. "Perhaps we should start by waking Snow White."

The L'Hovian prince nodded. "Let's get Prince Damian off to his not-quite-dead bride. But first, let's be sure your brother and retinue don't attack us first." He waved a man over. "I'll send a messenger. And we will gather up and go find your girl."

I frowned at the unexpected pain in my chest. We were closer than ever to my goal. Why wasn't I happier?

Chapter Twenty-Two

The Queen

Present day

I marked our steady approach to the Thwarven mining ridge with a growing ball of solid lead in my stomach.

Closer to my country's salvation.

Closer to my curse.

Closer to the one I had hated. That I had...tolerated...once.

Damian asked a few more questions about the princess, looking almost as pale and bloodless as I felt. His thumb threaded repeatedly over the horn of his saddle, wearing it to a yellow-brown under the dark dirt and grime.

My mind drifted back to the princess, and I remembered her haughty distance. Her silence. How easily she had withdrawn her love from me. But now, I wondered if I had seen it rightly after all. I had already been mistaken about L'Hovat. What if I was wrong about the princess too? What if she was just a victim, as I was? What could a child do under the weight of her father's thumb? How could I blame her if she, too, did it all to survive his brutality just as I did?

Her blue eyes shone more brightly in my memories. I could still almost feel her sloppy kisses on my cheek. The tickle of her tiny fingers in my palm. Her thick black tresses that I plaited nightly. Her yearning-filled glances, even as she grew up and grew away. The sound of her voice. Her nickname for me...

My heart ached, torn in two.

Because I had loved her once.

I had sent the huntsman first to avoid going myself. I had used poison instead of a dagger because I knew I couldn't actually stab her when it came down to it. But I needed to protect my crown and position from her father's post-mortem reach. Part of me wondered if I hadn't truly known that the Sleeping Death was a sleeping potion rather than a poison—a subconscious self-sabotage.

Because, despite it all, I loved her still.

"My lady?"

I wrenched my head up and toward the sound. "Oh, Damian. Er, Prince Damian. I'm sorry."

"You looked lost in thought."

Lost was one word for it. "I was thinking of the princess. I hope we can wake her."

He froze for a moment before speaking. "I am glad our nations might be brought together in peace."

I narrowed my eyes at the catch in his voice, like there was a hidden meaning in the words he spoke. But his face betrayed nothing.

His dark hair glinted in the midday sun, the unshaven stubble shadowing his sharp, angled jawline. His spine stood erect and steady as he rose with a particular masculine grace. Even disheveled from our difficult night, he looked every bit a prince. Powerful. Dangerous.

And yet, I felt so utterly drawn to him. So...

Seen, and yet so safe.

My stomach swayed uneasily. The prince would marry the princess. Our countries would be mutually benefited. I would be freed.

But then, why did my heart hurt so much?

A gathering of Zafmet men and Thwarven miners stood on the high ridge in front of us.

"Damian!" Caiden stood out against the crowd, waving frantically before he raced down the hill on foot. The others moved aside, revealing the glass casket of Snow White. I froze, holding my horse back. The rest of the men passed me as I gaped. She was there. Atop the hill. Moments away.

Damian moved toward his brother, hopping down to embrace him. Caiden pointed to her casket, smiling and babbling incomprehensibly. My breath caught in my throat. My vision narrowed. Soon Damian would go up there and kiss her. Soon I would face the consequences of my actions. Soon I would lose Damian to her forever.

I couldn't do this.

I whirled the horse around and kicked her to a trot.

"Lady?"

I glanced over my shoulder toward Damian, and I waved airily behind me. "Oh. I just can't watch. I...I couldn't bear it if it didn't work out as it should. Go to the princess. I will wait here for the news!" My voice sounded wound and tight. Kicking the horse again, I sped into a copse of tall white birch trees. The leaves clattered like the rain as the summer sun drove through their fluttering dance. The forest was happy for Snow and Damian too. Stupid forest. May the Fates' flames burn it all and me with it. I was a fool.

I dismounted, haphazardly tied the horse, and collapsed to the ground with my back against a trunk.

How had it come to this? How had he broken through my careful defenses? How could my heart betray me like this? I had a country to run, not an infatuation to entertain. I had a marriage to arrange and a trade to establish. Besides, he didn't know the real me. He couldn't.

Reaching past the broken vials, I snatched the cracked mirror from my bag and held it up to my face. Already, subtle red hues were becoming visible beneath the magicked blonde. My blue eyes glittered dimly through these dark green ones, and my nose looked longer, sharper. Only I could tell, but the effect of the potion was wearing off.

Soon, Damian would have his princess. All would be well. I would have fixed everything. We could marry them right here. Although... What if he refused to marry her once he knew who I really was? Would she go through with it once she saw it was me? Would the princes cancel their agreement when they learned of my deception?

The thoughts stabbed my heart. He had to marry her. He had to. For my people.

He couldn't marry her.

He would, though. Just as I planned.

I snorted bitterly. Oh, yes. My plans had all worked out so well: Become queen. Marry the king. Embarrass the king. Rule the country. Kill the princess. They had all been such raging successes.

As clearly as my true form slipped through this façade, the decades of artifice faltered and crumbled. I had believed I was the victim, and in many ways, I had been. But what had I done when I'd finally gained freedom from my oppressor, from the tyrant, from the king?

Murder.

I had become a murderer, in intent if not deeds. Just like him.

Furthermore, I had become an incompetent leader whose general, apparently, was running sieges in foreign lands without my knowledge or consent. Whose country was divided from within by fire and flood, by intolerance and my mismanagement.

I did not deserve to be queen. Did not deserve Damian.

Desolate, I pulled up my reflection again. "Mirror, mirror, in my hand, who is the fairest in the land?"

"Still stuck on that, are we?" the thousand voices hissed. Then they sighed, their sound like a gust through the trees. "Though she were asleep up there, the maiden who wakes is all that is fair."

I breathed out. "She's awake. She lives." Tears bubbled to the surface, spilling hot on my cheeks. "I'm so relieved. I'm so glad." Damian. My heart clenched again. "I hope they will be happy." I wished it to be so. Damian was a good man. Snow should have happiness. I could give her that at least. I owed her for almost killing her.

"Do you want to know what else I see?" the mirror asked.

I bit my lip, terrified, yet I nodded for it to continue.

"Though brittle and hard, sits someone lovely still. Whose softened heart is backed by obsidian will. Great strength, my queen, yet lies in you. To conquer or care, both sides are true."

I sobbed, and my head dropped down between my hands. "Mirror, I don't deserve to be queen."

From behind me, a voice spoke. "I don't agree."

Chapter Twenty-Three

The Queen

Present day

I leapt up and whirled around, the mirror clenched in my fist. Damian stood at the edge of the tall white trees, leaning one shoulder against its chalky bark.

"Damian. I—I mean Prince Damian. Congratulations on your nuptials."

"Oh." He took one step toward me. "But I am not yet engaged."

The words were slow to sink in. My heart thumped. Then thumped again.

I yanked up the mirror. "Mirror, who kissed the princess?"

"He who loves the princess bequeathed her a kiss. The man and savior appears like this." A vision filled the mirror of Caiden spinning in a field of wildflowers with Snow White draped across his arms. They were surrounded by Thwarven miners and forest creatures, all cheering and crying and holding each other as they laughed.

My hand slipped over my lips. "Caiden," I whispered.

"He fell in love with the princess along the way. Captured by the stories you told him on our journey. Solidified by her beauty and the love of her Thwarven friends." Damian stepped slowly to me. At each footfall, my heart rate increased, and my muscles tightened. He continued, the color of his bright green-blue eyes clear and too close. "I, unfortunately, did not feel any such sentiments for her."

"No?" I stepped back, but the trees were dense, and my spine landed on a trunk. "I'm...I'm sorry. Perhaps we can talk to the q-queen about the treaty."

"Your Majesty, the treaty is satisfied." Damian stopped an arm's reach away. "Unless, the queen refuses such an arrangement?" His gaze was piercing...and amused.

My breath caught, the blood leeching from my cheeks. "You knew?"

"There are many stories of Acacia's magic and the queen's shapeshifting. I had always thought them old wives' tales, myself. The recent reports were even more impossible. How could the most beautiful queen in an era transform into a wizened old crone? Yet..." He took one step forward, stealing all the air from the forest. "While you were not a very convincing lady-in-waiting"—his hand threaded a wisp of hair behind my ear—"you acted like a queen." He pulled up my hand and brushed his thumb against my obsidian ring. He looked sheepish for a moment. "Also, Johannes recognized your ring from when he was a boy. He said he'd watched you make it. But I had already figured it out by then."

The boy in the garden. "Little John," I whispered, sputtering, unmoored. "You knew." My cheeks burned. From his scorching gaze, or the heat in my belly, or the shame of my past, I was not sure. I tried to draw my hand back, but he held it gently. "I-I'm not a good person, Damian." A tear seared down my cheek. "I'm damaged. Broken."

His other thumb caught the tear and whisked it away. "Perhaps, like any soldier, you have scars and wounds. Perhaps you have nightmares and bear burdens that each soldier carries after seeing, doing, and being victim to atrocities that no human should bear." His face looked too familiar with his words. "Perhaps—"

"I poisoned the princess." The words tumbled out, and I clenched my fingers into fists, bracing myself for his rejection and horror.

But Damian just smiled. "She told us." My heart stopped. "And perhaps, you owe the princess an apology." My mouth popped open. He took a deep breath. "I won't pretend to understand if there are other wrongs you have to right or that everything will now be easy. But as I see it—from what I can tell, you are a survivor. You have endured. You were broken but did not shatter. You held yourself together bit by bit, even with all the odds stacked against you."

I opened my mouth to interrupt again, but he placed one finger as softly as a breath upon my lips. "And when confronted with your own misunderstandings, you listened and created solutions. When faced with the past, you spoke logically and with compassion. It is clear that you care for your people, even if you don't know all the details of how to run your country quite yet." He tilted his head. "Not to mention that it sounds like you were deliberately sabotaged in your dealings with L'Hovat..." I nodded. His smile broadened. "The fact remains that while I came to undo a curse and save a princess, I began to fall for her lady-in-waiting." Damian winked. "To fall for a queen. To fall for you."

Grasping both hands in mine, he leaned forward. "And as soon as your magic wears off, I look forward to getting to know the real you. All of you."

My voice wavered, unbelieving. "Even the broken pieces?"

"I will learn to love those too."

The tears fell unceasingly as I leaned my head onto his warm, safe shoulder and clasped his strong hands. The burden of being perfect, beautiful, competent, or even *good enough* clattered from my shoulders like a rockslide. The vulnerability was immense and terrifying, but it also felt freeing, like I was breathing for the first time in my life.

With a wave of my fingers, the obsidian stone began to glow. I whispered the words, and in a flash, the rest of the illusion spell dissipated.

Magic rushed back from my chest to every fingertip, I sighed in relief. When I looked back up at Damian, I was all me. My wild red curls were chaos in the wind, and he plucked at them to bounce them with a soft smile. Then, pushing my hair aside, he held my face in his hands, his eyes focused on mine.

"There you are." Damian's voice was soft, reverent. The tip of his finger brushed the end of my nose. I was seen.

"Mama Kiva?" The voice, still so sweet, drifted on the wind.

Ice slid down my back at her voice, and I leaned around Damian as he turned. Caiden approached, his hand intertwined with Snow White's. Her face, yet eighteen, was still as youthful as when she was nine. As when she was my girl too. With a whimper, I stepped, then all but ran to her, and fell to my knees before her, holding her hand in my own.

"Snow, please forgive me. I'm so sorry. I was...I was...horrible. The worst of fools. And I do not deserve your forgiveness, but I ask for it anyway."

She squeezed my fingers before she knelt with me. "Mama Kiva, I already have. I am sorry too. I should have never said anything to Father. I should have..." she whimpered. "Father was a bad man." Diamond tears fell down her perfect face. I wiped one away with my grimy fingertips. "Mama Kiva, I love you."

"Oh, Snow." I grasped her in a tight hug. Rejecting and aching to soak in her forgiveness. Too guilty to accept it but dying from thirst for her love. In our embrace, the past drifted into silence, and quietly, we connected as we had before. Our shared suffering now served as a bond rather than a dividing force between us. My jealousy dissipated like smoke from ash.

What a fool I was to hate this child who was as much a victim as I was.

As we sniffed, we parted, and I placed a hand on her cheek. "Snow, I love you too. Even when I was blinded by selfishness and fear and desperation. I always have."

Snow rose and tucked herself under the arm of a flushed and beaming Caiden. And I found myself turning back to Damian. He stood beside me, patient and waiting. He smiled. And for the first time in a long time, my heart flickered with the foreign sensation of soft affection. I pressed back into his side and felt his large hand settle on the small of my back.

It was so different, his touch. Instead of fear, I felt bolstered. Instead of pain, there was gentleness. Instead of insults, there could be guidance. Instead of selfishness, perhaps there could be love.

I had a lot of growing to do and more wounds to heal than I could enumerate. But now that I had stopped hemorrhaging, and killing myself with jealousy and desperate acts, perhaps I could be restored.

Perhaps I could be cared for.

Perhaps I could be whole.

Perhaps I could even be loved.

I smiled at the thought.

CHAPTER TWENTY-FOUR

The Mirror

Eight months later

I am the Mirror, and the truth is clear,

Souls are bound up by envy and fear.

The queen is now free by forgiveness from hate,

Starting anew with mercy's fresh slate.

The weeks of holding court are long. But the people now arrive in droves to see the silent queen who now speaks true words and the princess who was learning to rule Acacia. The queen has been teaching the princess everything she knows. Along with a new, scarred general, the queen has hired scores of her own people to run the castle and solve their local issues together. The people also come because rumors of the queen's equitable judgment and the renewed peace accords with their neighbors spread along with new waves of work, income, and trade. They do not love her, but they still need to see her for themselves.

She rests in her room after holding court. She holds me in her hand, though I see all from every wall and hall.

I tell her all I see, reflected simply, objectively, and carefully.

I won't be mistaken again.

As she heads toward the garden door, Yates calls to her. "Your Majesty?"

She turns with her lips pulled to one side. Gentle, but corrective. "Yates, we have discussed this."

The man stands taller. "We are yet in public."

"There is no one here now." She crosses her arms and leans heavily on one hip. "Try again."

Yates sputters and coughs. "K-Kevali." His face flushes a bright apple color.

"Yes, Yates?" The queen's smile crinkles her eyes into beautiful almonds, with folds on either side that carry her mirth.

"He is here."

Her eyes fly wide open. "Why didn't you say so? Where is he? How do I look? Never mind."

Tossing me in her pocket, she runs through the halls and the throne room and throws open the doors before Yates can catch up to her. On the other side stand Prince Damian and his men.

"Damian!" The queen runs and jumps into his arms. He lifts her up above everyone as he spins before setting her down in front of him.

"My dear queen, you are a welcome sight."

The queen's grin is as wild as her hair as she clasps his hands. The obsidian ring now hangs from a chain at her neck. "Close enough to remember the strength it took to survive, but far enough not to worship the wounds that made it," she had told me. Now, a clear, radiant gem casts a rainbow of light from her finger. A gift from the prince.

The two turn down the hallway as Damian disperses the men with a wave. They peel out to their rooms, joking and noisy and rough-housing as they go. The castle is alive. Happy.

"Have you already seen the newlyweds?" she asks as she pulls him to the gardens. Baby brush swallows cry and chirp from the flowering bushes along the stair.

Damian makes an unprincely snort. "Definitely newlyweds. If I hear another ballad, poem, or twinkling aria of their love, I may cut my own ears off."

The queen's laugh is music all its own.

Through one of my other mirrors, I spy the prince and princess in their manor across the park. Equally happy. Equally in love. A little naïve, but willing to work and forgive...or so they claim. Time and trials will tell.

The coronation is set, and soon the queen will crown the princess and her prince the monarchs of this land. Soon, she will return with Damian to rule over their nation together as queen with her king. Even after proving herself here, she will have a clean slate, a new castle, a fresh start. A true home.

At this point, if I could sigh, I might. The queen is finally thriving, alive in soul as well as body. The queen is finally happy, finally at peace. And she is loved by and loves a good man. The queen is no longer obsessed with being queen. She is Kevali.

Perhaps, as her hair spins around her, curled and wild and free from its binds and strict expectations, as her steps skip so lightly and unburdened, and as her heart glitters from her chest through her crinkled eyes, so brimming and full...

I am happiest to see that, finally, the queen sees her own value, treasures herself for who she is, and finally, *finally*, she loves herself.

Acknowledgements

This book has been a work in progress, in a few version. At first 30k, then 20k, and now back up to 28k, the progress has been a refining of author skills. The result is that this book has nestled itself deep in my heart.

So many people have been involved that I am afraid I am missing some...

But to my earliest readers: Constance, Rachel, Becky, Sara, to my latest: Celeste, and Alice and Kate, you all have helped blossom this limping creation into something, in my humble opinion, worth reading. I am so grateful for each of you and your time and your thoughts. Your smallest recommendations made reverberating changes. To Courtney who created the anthology that inspired it all.

To my husband, who is very much a Damian, who loves me when I'm a challenge to love, and calls me to be a better person. I'm grateful you found me.

To my God, the ultimate redeemer of blackened and broken hearts. Thank you for never giving up on us. Thank you for hearts of flesh, not stone. Every truth chime is your own making. I hope I reverberated them well enough to represent your persistent and pervasive love.

To write books for you is a great gift. Thank you to my readers who read, and feel and share in the story with me.

About the Author

Alora Carter is a native Coloradan sun-child who would rather be lost in a forest than adulting. She has two vibrant littles and a handsome viking-esque husband, as well as two wild German Shorthaired Pointers, a frog and four-foot corn snake named Sancho. Currently thriving in the lake lands of the mid-west, she finds herself through writing fantasy that sprinkles in cool science alongside themes of endurance in hardship, love conquers all, found family and growing the hidden potential in us all.

She began writing amidst the Pandemic in fall of 2021 and finished May 2022 with her first draft. Working nearly full-time and mothering full-time means she sneaks in minutes and hours to write and work on the next novel. She loves the imaginative human soul and hopes someone feels and grows with her along the way.

Spoiler alert: Good wins and love conquers all, even if it might not look like it at the time.

Website: www.AloraCarter.com

Facebook at www.facebook.com/AuthorAloraCarter

Instagram at www.instagram.com/AuthorAloraCarter

TikTok at https://www.tiktok.com/@AuthorAloraCarter

Goodreads at https://www.goodreads.com/author/show/2185065
0.Alora_Carter

Bookbub:https://www.bookbub.com/authors/alora-carter

Also By Alora Carter

The Awakened Prince - Clean Sleeping Beauty retelling with romance, snarky animal companions, evil vs good and love conquers all

Written with Rachel Rener, this heart warming story is worth reading and rereading again and again.

Free on my website when you join my newsletter!

1983. Dam Failure. Can Titania find her purpose when everything she planned is swept away?

Reviews and Typos

Indie or self publishing is a wonderful way to get my heart out on paper to people like you. Thank you so much for sharing your thoughts and feelings on your favorite review sites. It means the world to us wee author-types.

Also! If you find errors, typos or other mistakes, please email me directly at authoraloracarter@gmail.com. Don't mark them on Am.z as an "error" because badness will happen to me and the books!

Thank you!!!

You're the best.

Alora

www.ingramcontent.com/pod-product-compliance
Lightning Source LLC
Chambersburg PA
CBHW020413130626
46549CB00006B/2539